HIDDEN WEAPON

Shelter Morgan lay in the shadow of the cave for a long while, trying to remember. A pain shot through his lower back and he recalled it all suddenly. The five-thousand, the treachery, the long climb and the short fall. The woman . . .

"Kolka," Shell said out loud.

"God damn!" she said, and Shell laughed. She had been sitting in the shadows, and now she rose to walk to him, to peer into his eyes.

"I'm all right," Shell said.

There was no answer. Kolka touched his forehead, her hand cool and competent. Shell's weapons had been placed near at hand. Kolka indicated them, scooting the Colt nearer. She was a wise woman for one so young, knowing that Morgan needed that security right now with the killers on his backtrail.

One wounded man and a squaw—against an outlaw gang. He couldn't move fast and he couldn't fight hard. He had no cards.

"Wait till dark," Morgan said "and we'll have at it."

#19

SHELTER

THE HARD MEN

PAUL LEDD

ZEBRA BOOKS
KENSINGTON PUBLISHING CORP.

ZEBRA BOOKS

are published by

Kensington Publishing Corp.
475 Park Avenue South
New York, N.Y. 10016

First printing: August, 1984

Printed in the United States of America

1.

The first one rose up out of the yellow boulders, grinning with eagerness as he leveled his shotgun at the lone-riding, lanky gringo. The grin was washed away by a wave of horrible pain as he realized that the intended victim on the trail below had drawn his holstered Colt, turned smoothly in the saddle and fired, the .44-40 bullet slamming into the bandit's guts, pulping flesh and gristle, shattering bone, severing arteries. The bandit was blown backwards into the massive yellow boulder behind him, his unfired shotgun clattering free.

Gunsmoke lifted from Shelter Morgan's Colt revolver. The echo rolled through the long canyon. Beside him the bandit slid down the rocks, smearing them with the red of his shattered body.

Morgan didn't even see him. He had discounted that one the instant his first bullet tagged him. He was dead.

Still on his feet, perhaps, but dead.

Shelter's attention was already on the second outlaw and the third. Damn them all, he swore silently. All these little men with guns in their hands, all of them who had to travel in packs before they could dredge up anything like a man's courage from their cowardly guts.

Shelter had had a bellyfull of *bandidos*, of would-be killers, of back stabbers and ambushers these last weeks. He had nearly bought it in Baja, had crossed the unmarked border into California with a noticeable sense of relief. Jacumba was his goal, a small, desolate village high in the rocky hills beyond the Laguna Mountains east of San Diego.

There was business to be done there, dirty business, and he had no patience with these highwaymen and their kind. They waved a gun and you were supposed to stop, give them all you had, be humiliated, robbed and then probably shot anyway. They had chosen the wrong victim this time.

Shelter's Colt bucked in his hand again and the man in the big sombrero who had been blocking the trail was spun around, his rifle discharging into the ground, his cry of pain, of panic reaching Morgan's ears. He tried to crawl off the trail, his dragging leg sketching a crooked furrow in the sandy soil between the upthrust pillars of rock.

The third one rode a pinto pony. His hat was dangling down his back, tethered by a rawhide string. He was good, and almost very lucky.

"Hold it, *amigo!*" he shouted, and the rifle in his fists exploded. It wasn't a well-aimed shot, but it was damned close. The bullet notched the ear of the big gray horse Morgan rode and the gelding reared up in confusion,

6

throwing Shell's aim off badly.

Morgan's answering shot struck rock and ricocheted off down the long canyon. The bandit on the pinto levered a fresh round into the chamber. His eyes glinted with pleasure and he managed a broken-toothed grin of triumph. He had his man, had the lean *gringo*. The others might be dead—so what? He would not have to split the contents of the *gringo*'s saddlebags with anyone. Maybe there was silver or gold in those saddlebags, enough so that Ramon Flores y Cantada—that was the bandit's name—would not have to work for many months.

Ramon despised work. He hadn't worked since the day he had hit the fat man over the head and taken his pistol from him. He had been sixteen then.

Ramon was too busy fantasizing. He was too pleased with himself, too self-satisfied. In his mind he had already killed the *gringo*, found much silver in the saddlebags and returned south to spend it on tequila and women.

He had forgotten one important bit of business—the *gringo* wasn't dead.

Ramon saw the big gray buck and toss its head, go up on hind legs and paw at the air. Behind the horse, lying inert and blood stained on the trail, Ramon noticed Angel, but he wasn't concerned about his friend's death. A friend was someone you used; when he was of no use any longer he was no longer your friend.

"Madre de Dios!"

Ramon had been waiting for a shot at the *gringo* who had been clinging to the horse's mane, shielding himself with the horse's body, Indian-fashion, but when the gray settled, the *gringo* was gone!

Ramon looked around, his eyes widening with terror,

7

then he threw himself toward the cover of the nearby rocks, making it just as a bullet struck the rockface beside his head, showering him with stone splinters. His horse galloped away.

Ramon took a few seconds to cross himself as his mother had taught him to do. A man never knew . . . he looked around frantically and began to climb.

He clawed at the rough yellow granite, scrambling madly up the stack of boulders. The sun had heated the rocks and they burned his fingers. Sharp outcroppings split the skin over his knees and elbows painfully. Sweat ran into his eyes, burning them.

Above him somewhere was the blue sky, the yellow sun—and below him was the crazy *gringo* with the Tiger Colt. Ramon climbed, not daring to look back across his shoulder. Down there was the place where men died. Down there was the *gringo*.

He could see the notch in the rocks above him now, see the white sunlight streaming through it. If he could reach the ledge he could scramble down into the little valley beyond. He knew the way from there, the way no one could follow. If he could only . . . and then Ramon's heart skipped to a stop before beginning a long, dreadful pounding which lifted his pulse so that it banged against the top of his skull, so that his ears rang with it.

The tall dark silhouette was pasted against the blue-white sky above him.

Tall, lean, clad in jeans and a cotton shirt, hatless now so that the somewhat long dark hair shifted in the dry desert breeze—and dangling from his hand was that Colt, that dreadful pistol which missed nothing it was aimed at.

"Señor . . ."

"Come on up, *bandido*," the soft voice invited.

"I was not with them. I was a prisoner . . ."

"Keep climbing, *compadre.*"

"I thought you were an outlaw! Isn't that so funny? Heh? I thought you were a *bandido*!" There was hysteria in Ramon's voice now, hysteria as he realized he wasn't even convincing himself with his flimsy lies.

"Climb or I'll shoot you off the rocks," the too-soft voice instructed. The man was crouched down now, hands dangling between his legs.

"I have no gun," Ramon said, hoping the *gringo* could not see his pistol which was thrust behind his waistband in front.

"Then I'll give you one," Shelter Morgan answered, and the voice was no longer so soft. "Get up here, my friend. You've tried to kill me. You screwed it up. Now you're going to have to pay for the mistake."

"You cannot *kill* me!" The voice was terrified, high-pitched. "You cannot just shoot me!"

"No? Why not? You were going to shoot me."

"Yes, but that is different . . ."

"Climb, *hombre,* climb on."

Ramon did, his fingers numb with the fear of death, his legs heavy, his heart, damn it!, pounding away so that he could not think, could not devise a way out of this. It was too far to jump now. He would only break himself against the rocks below.

The *gringo* wasn't going to believe any of his lies. Ramon knew that now. Usually they did. You could tell them anything. They tried to give you the benefit of the doubt. You could steal from them and then hold their possessions up in front of them and tell them they were your own, and they would believe you, trying to be fair! It was funny. Many times Ramon had laughed at the gullibility of the *gringos*. Now he was not laughing at anything.

He was within ten feet of the rimrock and the tall man rose to his feet again to stare down. Ramon couldn't see his face. He was just an angular dark silhouette against the glaring sky.

Perhaps . . . Ramon's mind worked desperately. If he could fool the man just a little, get the man to believe one little lie. It had always worked before.

"Please, señor, I beg you . . ." Ramon gasped. "I cannot make it up. I can climb no more."

"No?"

"No, señor, I cannot. Please—give me a hand up. *Por favor!*"

Ramon lifted a supplicating hand toward the dark figure. Ramon's right boot rested on a crumbling but firm ledge; below his left foot was a small rounded outcropping. He would have plenty of support. But the *gringo*—he would have no chance. If Ramon once got hold of that hand and pulled, the tall man would be yanked out into space to tumble to the rocks far below, and if the fall did not kill him Ramon's concealed pistol surely would.

"Por favor!" Outside Ramon's expression was pitiable, his wide mouth drooping sadly, his melancholy brown eyes damp and round. The fingers of his hand wriggled as they stretched toward Morgan. Inside the *bandido* was laughing. Laughing! The man was going to take his hand, was actually going to help him up!

Ramon made his move, snatching at the left wrist of the *gringo*, he braced himself and started to pull. But the *gringo* made his own move first.

Ramon saw the tall man's right hand move, felt the

sudden crushing blow as the barrel of the *gringo*'s Colt revolver smashed against Ramon's wrist. Bone cracked and incredible pain shot through the bandit's arm. Worst of all he *knew*.

He knew it was all over; knew that he was a dead man. He had already begun his own movement, movement meant to destroy the tall man. Bracing himself Ramon had gripped the *gringo*'s wrist and twisted his own body around and back violently, meaning to unbalance the *gringo*.

His shattered wrist was incapable of maintaining a grip, however, and the motion, already begun, could not be stopped. Ramon was still twisting, still flinging himself backward when his right boot lost its purchase on the crumbled stone underfoot.

He clawed at the air for a long moment, fighting for balance, not achieving it. He had time to focus on the silhouette of the tall man once more before he cartwheeled back into space, slamming off the yellow boulders below him, before he landed crumpled and broken against the sandy trail. There wasn't time to cross himself before the breath ran out completely.

Shelter Morgan stood looking, listening for a long moment before he holstered his gun and began climbing down. He found the gray and settled it, stroking its velvety neck. The day was hot even in the canyon shadows. Sweat stained Shelter's shirt at the armpits, on his back and chest as he moved to examine the dead.

There wasn't much to them. Little brown men with big hats and big guns. Their boots were run-down, their shirts patched and filthy. They weren't much, but they didn't deserve to be left to the buzzards either. Shelter laboriously loaded them onto their horses and tied them there, the sweat raining off him.

He stopped, removed his hat and wiped his brow. Then he shook his head.

They are always with us. The dead. There was no longer any fascination with death for Shelter Morgan—he had seen too much of it. But there seemed to be plenty of fascination for other people, the way they rushed toward it.

"There's a long time to be dead," Shell said softly. And too damned little time to be alive. He meant to enjoy that while he could. He wanted to walk in the sunlight, eat good beef, cool his thirst with icy spring water or cold beer which danced across the palate. He meant to lay himself down with a willing woman and cradle his tired body in her tender arms . . .

He looked at the dead men slumped over their horses' backs. "It sure as hell, gentlemen, beats the hell out of what you've purchased."

Jacumba sat on top of a broken, rock strewn tableland overlooking the flat, white desert beyond. Somewhere across the flats, just out of sight, lay the Colorado River, narrow and muddy this far south. To the north and east lay chocolate-colored mountains, stripped by eons of harsh weather, fluted by flash floods, desolate, naked, forbidding.

Jacumba itself consisted of two dozen buildings, over half of them made out of native stone. Not cut stone, but rounded rocks from boulder size at the foundations to cobblestone size at the eaves, all piled one on top of the other and roughly mortared.

There was a windmill standing almost in the center of

town, a stone well beside it where several baked, salt-streaked horses drank. A saloon was directly adjacent, across the street and up a ways a two story hotel which seemed monstrously out of place in this tiny village. Lining the street on the desert side was a close-growing colonnade of salt cedars planted there in a vain attempt to cut the searing east wind and shield the town from the sandstorms.

Down the main street Shelter Morgan rode, his horse and the trailing horses kicking up puffs of lime-colored dust. People had begun to peep out of their windows, to emerge from the shade to follow along.

"Did you kill 'em all, mister? Did you kill 'em all? Who are they?"

Shelter glanced at the lean, straw-hatted kid who ran beside him, chattering questions.

"You got a town marshal here, son?"

"A marshal, why you bet! Just Jeb Thornhill, what do you think of that?"

Shelter, who had never heard the name, didn't think much of it one way or the other. The kid obviously did. "Fine. Where is he?"

"He's at lunch, but the office is that way. You got to go around the corner. See—there, next to the hardware store."

Then the kid was asking his questions again. He wasn't the only one. A knot of Jacumba's citizens had formed and they trailed along: old women in bonnets, men with canes, in townsuits and overalls, dogs yapping excitedly. Shelter guessed they didn't have much excitement in this high desert community and they meant to make the most out of whatever came their way.

"Damn me, damn me for a Yankee if that ain't Ramon Flores," someone shouted.

"You're crazy, Ned."

"Crazy am I? Come closer. Think a dead man's going to bite you, Harper?"

Shelter reined up in front of the marshal's office already sick of the clamor. He hated the killing, he always had, but he disliked the rehashing even more, the telling of war stories. The anxious, blood-thirsty faces staring up eagerly, wanting every last bit of gore.

"I tell you it ain't Flores!"

Shelter sat his horse before the marshal's office, unmoving as the local people prodded the dead men, shooing away the flies.

It was ten minutes in the hot sun before the wide, white-shirted man wearing a broad straw colored mustache, riding a leggy sorrel horse sauntered down the dusty alley to the jailhouse.

His eyes were weather-cut. They had that look about them. The man had seen death and had dealt it out. The expression as he surveyed the dead was almost lugubrious. He shook his head as if the matter was intolerably sad. Then the eyes lifted to Shelter Morgan.

"You and me had better talk, I guess. Harvey, get these boys over to the coroner! Don't stand there gaping. Get along, now!"

The marshal inclined his head and Morgan swung down from the weary gray, hitching it loosely as the marshal, dismounting, let loose a heavy sigh.

"The rest of you folks can just clear out of here too," the lawman said wearily. "I only want to talk to one man." The marshal smoothly, unexpectedly slipped his Remington .44 from his holster. Those sad eyes were

14

fixed firmly on Shelter Morgan as he added, "And I want to speak to you without that gun."

"Marshal . . ."

"Please," the lawman said. He cocked his Remington, still looking very sad, very deadly. "Just drop that gunbelt of yours. If you don't, my friend, I'll shoot you where you stand."

2.

Those sad, sad eyes the marshal had fixed on Shelter Morgan didn't fool Shell a bit. He was up against a hard man here. If the marshal promised to shoot to kill, he meant it. He would quietly ask you to drop your gun and if you didn't comply he would shoot you dead, all without changing expression.

Shelter weighed the alternatives and unbuckled his belt very slowly.

"Good," the marshal said with a small, satisfied nod. "Now if you'll just turn and march into the jail. Straight on back through, if you please."

"Listen, marshal . . ."

"I'll do my listenin' inside." The marshal grunted as he leaned over to pick up Shell's gunbelt. "On inside now."

Shelter shrugged and walked up the single stone step to

16

the green door of the stone jailhouse. He walked on through, ducking the low lintel, into a musty, warm room.

"Straight back."

"I thought we were going to talk."

"We are. As soon as you've done what I told you," the marshal said. "Straight back."

Straight back was the single cell of the town jail. Iron bars set into heavy wooden frames rocked around securely. There was a single high window large enough for a squirrel to slip through—if he was a narrow squirrel.

"In the cell?"

"That's it, son."

Shelter went ahead, taking a slow deep breath, letting it out in one disgusted exhalation. He walked into the cell and heard the door bang shut behind him, heard the ratcheting of tumblers as a key was turned in the lock.

Shell turned slowly around. The marshal had holstered his pistol and was tugging his shirttails free of his trousers as he crossed the room to his wildly disordered desk.

"Now?" Morgan asked a little bitterly.

"Sure. Now," the marshal replied. "You go ahead and tell me all about it, son."

Marshal Jeb Thornhill apparently had his own way of doing things. He sat down at his desk and began leafing through the stacks of paper on it in an apparently random manner, lifting his eyes to Shelter only occasionally as Morgan told in a simple, straightforward way what had happened on the trail.

"And so you brung 'em in," Thornhill said when Shell was through. "Uh-huh, most admirable, I'd say."

"Then maybe you'd like to let me out, Thornhill."

"Maybe I would. Maybe I will—as soon as I finish going through these wanted posters, Mister . . . I don't recall you mentioning your name."

"Morgan, Shelter Morgan."

"That wouldn't be the name you were born with, would it?" the marshal asked. He was holding up a wanted poster, glancing from it to Morgan as they spoke. "How tall are you?"

"Six foot three."

"Way too tall for this fellow." The poster fluttered to the floor beside the desk.

"And yes, that's the name I was born with."

"Do tell?" The marshal scratched his head. "Here's one on Toby Crane. Do you believe that? They're still looking for that bastard and Herb Crane shot him dead down in Nogales two, three months back. I'll have to wire the US Marshal on that . . ."

"Marshal Thornhill!" Shelter was clinging to the black iron bars of the cell, the patience running out of him now. "Do you mind telling me what is going on here? Am I under arrest or what?"

"Under arrest?" The marshal scratched his head again. "No, I don't reckon."

"Why did you put me in here?"

"You want to know?" Thornhill shook his head and came to his feet, carrying a sheaf of wanted posters with him as he walked toward the cell. "I'll tell you, my friend. You were jumped by three very bad *hombres* out there on the grade. Very bad. And you just happened to kill every damned one of them. It wasn't luck that killed them, it was gun skill. You don't get lucky three times like that.

18

That indicates to me a very tough man, Mister Shelter Morgan, one that maybe has used a gun a time or two before."

"I'm not an outlaw."

"No—maybe not. But it doesn't mean anything to say it. I'm going to finish going through these wanted posters to make sure you're not an outlaw. That's doin' my duty, you understand? It don't hurt you none to sit in there and cool your heels. It don't hurt you none to let your iron over here cool off a little. Just sit there and take it for a time more, Mister Shelter Morgan."

"There isn't much else I can do, is there?"

"No, son, there ain't."

Shell sat down on the bunk which was suspended from chains imbedded in the stone wall. As a mental exercise he studied the cell, deciding it wasn't as break-proof as they probably hoped. Not for a determined man.

By the time he was finished with that the marshal was done with his posters, most of which ended up strewn across the floor.

"Well, Mister Morgan, I can't find a thing on you." The marshal stretched. "All the same, I wouldn't object if a man like you was to drift on sooner rather than later. I don't like killing."

"I don't like it either," Shell said as the marshal reached for the keyring on the wall and walked to the cell door. "But as for the leaving—it might be a little while, maybe longer than either of us would wish."

"That so?" The marshal's voice was almost disinterested, but Shelter could sense an intense interest in the lawman's words. "Care to tell me why it is you're in Jacumba, Mister Shelter Morgan?" he asked as he swung the door open and stepped back, letting Shelter pass

19

through. Even then Thornhill let his hand rest close to his holstered pistol. The marshal was no fool. He would probably live for a good long time.

"I did ask you a question," Thornhill prompted.

"Yes. The answer is, no I don't care to tell you why I came to Jacumba."

"Bad business then."

"You make too many assumptions, marshal. You're a suspicious man." Shelter picked up his gunbelt from the marshal's desk and clipped it around his waist, buckling it on.

"You're right there, Morgan, I am a suspicious man. I'll have my eye on you, you know. Any trouble and it won't be an eyeblink before you're back in the can. I don't trust a man who has to hide things from me."

Shelter turned around, smiling. He looked Marshal Thornhill in the eye and touched his hat brim. "Goodbye. Thanks for everything. By the way—never heard of a man called Joe Bass have you?"

Thornhill couldn't hide it. The question stung him somewhere, in a way Shelter couldn't guess at. Thornhill went pale beneath his deep tan and his eyebrows drew together sharply.

"What was that name?"

"Joe Bass."

"What's your interest in Joe Bass?"

"You know him?" Shelter responded.

"I didn't say that, Morgan. I was just curious."

"I know—you don't like anyone hiding anything from you." Shell said with a grin.

"Still right." Thornhill's voice was a little colder now. "I've got my job to do and people to protect."

"Including Joe Bass?"

"I don't recollect saying I ever heard of the man."

"All right. We're not going to get far with this, are we?"

"Not unless you loosen up, Morgan." The marshal opened the jailhouse door. Harsh, dry light streamed through, patching the floor. "Another damned sandstorm getting up out on the flats," the marshal commented. "We get an east wind like that we're bound to get sand."

And there was a wind blowing, a dry, demon wind that curled everything up at the corners, withered it and blew it away. Thornhill tried one more time.

"I don't recollect you telling me what you wanted this Joe Bass for. A working job, was it? Because if it was, there's better jobs around close to Jacumba."

"Are there? No, it's not a job I want, marshal—it's personal business I have with Joe Bass." Shelter swung up on the big gray's back and sat in the saddle for a moment, hands on the pommel, leaning forward toward Jeb Thornhill.

Shelter said, "You say there are better jobs close in to Jacumba—does that mean you know where Joe Bass is?"

"No." Thornhill turned his head and spat. "I don't know a thing about him. I don't know where he is. If you find out, Morgan, you make sure you come by and tell me, won't you?"

"A man you don't even know?" Shelter grinned. "Why, marshal, that doesn't make a deal of sense to me. What business would that be of yours?"

Then with a dry chuckle Shelter backed the gray from the hitch rail, turned up the street and with the dry desert wind at his back he rode toward the hotel.

The tall cedar trees shook in the wind. As Shell turned

the corner he could see the sand moving out on the desert below. Like low clouds drifting toward the rocky foothills. Leaves and loose papers cartwheeled and shuttled past before the hoofs of the big gray horse. A sign painted on canvas fluttered against the general store, making snapping noises. The windmill in the heart of town was spinning like a top, whining and creaking. Someone would have to climb it and put the brake on, Shelter thought.

There were a dozen big oaks around the Jacumba Hotel. These and the jumbled boulders which rose up around it, forming a broken teacup valley, shielded it from the brunt of the wind. Nevertheless Shelter was aware of it, drying his perspiration-dampened shirt, tugging at his hat, kicking up the light dust as he swung down before the wooden porch of the great stone hotel, wrapped the gray's reins loosely around the iron hitching post, slipped his saddlebags and climbed the steps.

And there she was. Right behind the hotel desk, wide-eyed, pert, small with delightful rounded breasts, a full lipped smile, sleek dark hair done up in ringlets which bounced as she moved. She wore calico and lace and her eyes grew even more friendly, brighter as she turned to Shelter Morgan.

"Yes, sir?"

"Shelter."

"Yes, we can shelter you," she replied.

"My name. My name is Shelter, not 'sir'." He had placed his saddlebags on the counter and now, tilting his hat back, he positioned his elbows on it as if he were going to be there for a long, long while.

"Yes . . . well," she was smiling still, but there was some confusion in her pretty blue eyes. "If you'll sign the book then . . . you are a guest?" she asked, suddenly unsure of everything.

"Yes, I'm a guest. You didn't ever tell me your name," Shelter said, taking the pen from the lady, dipping it in the deep violet ink in the well beside him.

"I am Miss Richardson," she answered. "I'll be your hostess while you are at the Jacumba Hotel . . ."

"I didn't get your name," Shelter said, glancing up again, handing her the pen which she took gingerly.

"Why, I just told you . . ."

"That's no kind of name. If I tell you I'm Mister Morgan that immediately sets up a rather formal relationship, don't you think? So I didn't say that to you. I told you who I am—Shelter. You see?" He grinned and she backed away a little, looking around the empty lobby.

"Yes, I think so."

"And so you'll have to give me another name, you see."

"It's something I don't like to give out," she stammered.

"Too shy?"

"Something like that. People laugh."

"They do what?"

"Laugh at my name."

"I wouldn't. I promise you that."

She looked around the lobby once more, touched her dark hair nervously and then said hesitatingly, "It's Merriweather. Merriweather Richardson."

"So folks call you Merri."

"Yes, they do. But they never spell it right. It's a nuisance. All of my records, even my birth certificate, are wrong . . . why here I am talking to you as if I know you, and I don't at all, do I, Mister Morgan?"

23

"Not yet you don't," Shell said and he winked, picking up his saddlebags. "Got a key for me?"

"Yes." Her ears were reddening as she turned away. Charming, Morgan thought. Very charming. She found a key on a leather fob and handed it to him. "Sixteen—you didn't say, do you want a bath too?"

"Yes. Definitely a bath. I'd also like to have a kid come up and get a list of things I need from the general store—a clean shirt and such. You have somebody who can do that for me?"

"Yes. Abraham. He's an Indian, a Tipai boy. He'll be happy to do it for a little change."

"Good. Dinner here?"

"Yes, we serve dinner."

"I mean, will you have it with me, Merri?"

"I couldn't . . . no, not tonight. I just couldn't. Thank you, but no."

"I'll order for two and hope you can change your plans. What do you like best?"

"I usually have the stuffed pork chops, but I won't be there, I just can't!"

"I'll order pork chops and pretend you are there," Shelter said with a crooked little smile. "At eight o'clock I'll start doing that. If you happen to walk by and see a man sitting in your dining room, talking sweet talk to a woman who isn't there, that'll be me. And if you don't want me to embarrass the hotel, why maybe you'll come over and sit down and let me talk to you instead."

With that he was gone, leaving the slightly befuddled girl to stare after him. Merriweather Richardson felt like her head was filled with feathers, her belly filled with soft warm pudding. The tall man with the blue eyes—why, he was a fast one, a flirt.

24

And very handsome. Very sure. Shaved, with a clean shirt on . . . Merri shook her head. What was she thinking of! She got back to work but she caught herself filing mail in the wrong pigeonholes and once just standing there staring at the stairwell across the lobby where Shelter Morgan had disappeared.

Morgan was enjoying a long, skin-reddening bath. The water was up to his neck. Only his head and his knees appeared above the steaming water as he slumped in the big copper tub.

At the tap at the door he called, "Come in," without turning his head.

It was Abraham. The Indian kid was under five feet tall though he was up into his early teens. His hank of blue-black hair was cropped off straight across his sloping forehead. His wide nose flared at the nostrils, giving the kid a slightly simian expression. He grinned as he came in, revealing a mouthful of pearly teeth.

"I got a fine shirt, very nice."

"Not too fancy."

"No, you said not too fancy. Just dark blue with diamond shape buttons. Very pretty, not too fancy." The kid threw the paper wrapped packages on the bed.

"You manage to get the shaving soap?"

"I got you everything you wrote down. I watched the man make a mark by everything," Abraham said. His education hadn't included reading, but he had been determined to do a good job.

"Socks?"

"Yes." The kid took a step closer. "I shine your boots for another dime."

"I don't know if those'll take a shine, Abraham," Shelter said doubtfully. He glanced at those boots, cracked and weather dried, down at the heel, almost colorless. He needed a new pair but that was one thing you couldn't let someone else buy for you. Abraham looked downcast. "Give it a try if you want," Shelter told him. "I'll give you a quarter if the polish sticks."

Abraham even got the polish to shine and Shelter gave him a whole dollar. At dusk as the rising wind pushed the sand up against the skirts of the hills and the dove flew homeward across purpling, orange-streaked skies, Shelter Morgan stood on the balcony of his hotel room wearing the new dark blue shirt and new-polished boots. His jeans had been washed, dried in the desert wind and slipped back on. The Colt which rode on his hip had been cleaned and oiled.

Morgan looked out over the town and nodded his head with satisfaction. He was ready. It was time to go man-hunting.

3.

No one glanced his way as the tall man walked through the green painted door, leaving the dust and wind of the outside for the cool semi-darkness of the saloon. The Red Dog, they called it. At least that was what the sun-blistered sign outside said. There were no red dogs in evidence when Shelter crossed the earthen floor of the saloon, glancing at the faces of the men illuminated only at intervals where the overhead oil lamps caught them.

The talk was a low constant murmuring; if a man listened closely he could make out individual words. Most of it was poker argot spiced with pungent American cussing.

Shelter eased up to the bar and rested an elbow there, his hat tilted forward, his foot propped up on the wooden rail.

"How many?" the bartender asked. They had whiskey

27

and nothing else.

"One tall one."

Shelter had been looking forward to a cool beer, would have much preferred it, but beer was a luxury the farther west you got, and in this country there just wasn't any way to keep it cool.

The whiskey, a third of a water glass, was placed before him, a dollar collected, and Shell was left to survey the Red Dog and its customers.

Howard Savage had told him about Jacumba. Savage had been sure, damned sure that Joe Bass was living there. And Savage had reason to know, to remember.

"Two years I served under that bastard," Savage had told him over some of the coldest beer in San Diego. "Captain Morgan, you never seen an officer the like of Joe Bass." Howard Savage shook his head. "I seen some bad ones, I seen some cowardly ones, but I never seen a plain vicious one like Major Joe Bass—how the hell he ever made that rank, I don't know. Couldn't of been regular Confederate army, come to think of it. He must have bought that commission."

"He did. South Carolina militia, Howard. He was a gentleman planter on Monday, a major on Tuesday."

"And a butcher on Wednesday," Savage said bitterly. He tried not to show the stump he had instead of a right hand but Morgan knew it was there, beneath the table. That was some of Major Joe Bass' wartime work—and not the worst of it.

"What happened, Howard?"

"Just a plain rantin' rage, Captain Morgan. We met a Yankee unit—Third Connecticut, it was—outside of Julesburg, Major Joe Bass commanding after Colonel Harry Lamp went down with a ball through the brisket."

"I recall Lamp. He was a good one."

"Damn right he was, Captain. One of the best. Well, he was a professional too, which Bass never was. When Colonel Lamp went down Major Bass tried to fill the colonel's boots. Fill 'em! Hell, he couldn't even walk in 'em. Got us cut off from the Eleventh, is what he did. Cut off back of Julesburg—were you there, Captain Morgan? No? Well, if it was two-to-one it was ten-to-one. It looked like a blue forest in the back hills. But Bass gets us in there and gets us cut off. By the time we made our own lines we were short one man in three, maybe more—and Bass who'd seen himself as some kind of Stonewall Jackson was frothing with rage. Just plain mad, sir. Me, I brought in the report that we were all done on the eastern flank and he stood there just glaring at me. Crazy in the eyes. Thing is, Joe Bass was crazy. I believe that. People didn't seem to realize that, but he was. I told him we had to withdraw again and he yanks that saber out and swipes at my face with it. Just like that—a crazy man. A reflex caused me to throw up my hand, I guess. Well," Savage shrugged, "there never was a hand worth a damn for stopping whetted steel."

"There's no doubt in your mind that he's in Jacumba."

"That's where the freight went, Captain Morgan." Savage was shipping agent for a freight company in San Diego. "Plain as day, inked on there nice and plain, 'Joe Bass, Jacumba, California'. Now, you ask me is it the same man, I don't know for a fact, but I was told by his brother once that he'd come to California."

"You talked to his brother?"

"Yes, sir, I did."

"Any particular reason?"

"Yes, sir, there was," Savage said, lifting his hand onto

the table. He nodded at the stump. "A man doesn't forget that easy. Now—well, maybe I'm a little older, a little more a coward, but I don't want to tangle with Joe Bass anymore. I'd be glad to see him get his, though, Captain. Happy as a hog in slop. If it is Joe Bass, and I think it must be, I'll be pleased if you'd speak my name to him once before you plug the bastard."

"I will try to remember to do that," Morgan promised.

"Me, I sort of lost touch with my hate, Captain." Savage looked into Morgan's deep blue eyes. He looked far into them and saw it. "You haven't lost yours though, have you? There's something powerful eating at you."

"That's right," Morgan admitted but he didn't feel like talking about it and Savage knew enough not to press it. They had another beer and then said goodbye, Shelter leaving Savage standing on a fog-shrouded dock as he rode slowly east, toward the desert hills.

"Haven't seen you around," the voice at Morgan's elbow said and he turned to see the withered man in faded coveralls scratching his chin as he studied Shell. "Or have I—dang it, yes I have! You're the man who killed Ramon Flores and a few of his Mex pals. Didn't know you with a shave and a shine. Hey, Andy! This here's the one that got Flores!"

Shelter winced. The last thing he had wanted was for attention to be focused on him. Andy and several of his card-playing cronies turned, interest on their faces. Fortunately the old man had a high, thin voice, and his words hadn't carried across the Red Dog.

"Let's find a quiet table," Shelter said, grabbing the old man's arm.

"Sure. You bet. I want to hear all about it." He grabbed a bottle as they left the bar and Shell guided him

30

roughly to a corner table where they sat in the shadows.

"What's your name?" Morgan asked.

"Clyde. Clyde Wilcox."

"All right. Look here, Clyde. I really don't want a big rumpus raised over me and this Flores business, you understand." Shell poured the old man a drink.

"Sure—kind of shy." Clyde leaned forward, winking heavily. "Got someone on your trail? I hear tell you're a gunfighter, and I figure you must be to have got them Mex *bandidos* that way."

"Something like that," Shelter agreed since it was the easiest thing to do. "So keep it under your hat, will you?"

"I will, but hell, partner, a lot of people saw you ride in this afternoon. People know who you are all right. A stranger stands out in a place like this, you know. Yep, they damn sure know who Shelter Morgan is."

"They all know my name too, do they?"

"Sure they do. There's no secrets in Jacumba. When somethin' juicy comes along, folks talk about it, don't you know? Any harm in people knowin' your name?"

"I don't know," Shell said. He turned his whiskey glass without looking at it, lifting it. It sure as hell wasn't going to help any for them to know who he was, that he was there. He had announced himself without meaning to—he should have left Ramon and his friends to the buzzards.

"I won't say anything else if it'll help," Clyde said conspiratorially. He winked again, filled his glass and hoisted the tumbler to Shelter. "Sorry I shot my face off, Morgan."

"That's all right. By the way," he said as casually as possible, "you don't happen to know a man named Joe Bass, do you, Clyde?"

31

Clyde didn't answer immediately. His eyes narrowed suspiciously. He swallowed twice; his hands tensed, Shell noticed, curling like talons reflexively. Clyde didn't like the question any more than the marshal had.

"I didn't catch the name."

"You caught it. Joe Bass. What's going on around here, Clyde? You afraid of Joe Bass? Is the town afraid of him?"

"Afraid?" Clyde scratched his chin. "No," he said, shaking his head, "I wouldn't say that. There's just some divided opinion about him, let me put it that way."

"Why's that?"

"Folks naturally have different opinions," Clyde said evasively. "I don't recall you sayin' why you wanted to find Joe Bass."

Shelter didn't answer that. "Where is he?" he asked, and his voice was soft but his eyes were cold, cold and hard as blue steel, Clyde Wilcox thought. Yes, this was a bad one. Shelter Morgan was the kind of man he had thought he was. The kind that could take Ramon Flores and a dozen more.

"That's an easy one to answer—I don't know where in hell he is," Clyde said.

The door to the saloon burst open and a light wash of sand drifted in. A young, blond haired, excited fellow came in with the dust.

"Posters are goin' up on Joe Bass!" he shouted to the saloon at large.

There was a scraping of chairs, glass being broken, an abrupt surge of conversation.

"Where at?" someone shouted.

"Sit tight, Hawkins. The marshal's on his way over here next."

"How much is on him?" someone else shouted.

"A thousand dollars."

"That's music to a man who just dropped his last eagle," the gambler said happily.

Shelter glanced toward the door then back to Clyde Wilcox who took a quick nervous drink of his whiskey and then shook his head with a touch of bitterness.

"What's the matter, Clyde?"

"Nothin', Morgan. I just never did like a coon hunt."

"A mob, you mean."

"I didn't say so—you're a part of it, aren't you?"

"If it's Joe Bass, I'm leading the way," Shelter told him honestly.

"That's what I thought . . ."

The door opened again and Jeb Thornhill stumped in, dust clinging to him, his slicker, hat and mustache thick with it. The men in the Red Dog got to their feet and surged forward as the marshal took one of the posters he carried beneath his arm and tacked it up on the saloon wall.

"Stand back, will you, boys," Thornhill said. "Please! Here. Here's an extra few posters—hand 'em around before I get trampled, damn it!"

The posters started circulating, an excited buzz growing as each man touched the wanted bill and touched in imagination the thousand-dollar reward that was being offered. Shelter had eased along the wall, elbowing his way through the mob until he was at the marshal's shoulder, reading the posted bill he had tacked to the wall.

"When do we leave, Marshal?"

Thornhill jerked around at the sound of Shelter's voice. He looked him up and down and shrugged.

"Not tonight, that's for damned sure. That sandstorm is whipping up good out there. No point in travellin', a man can't see and a horse can't breathe."

"And in the morning there won't be any tracks to see," Shelter pointed out.

The marshal looked at Shelter with an expression that might have been cynicism. "That's right, too, isn't it, Mister Morgan?"

"Kidnapping?" Morgan had only now gotten to the specifics on the wanted poster. "Who'd he snatch?"

"It's on there. Dorothy Patch. John Patch's daughter."

"His own sister!" Someone said from in back of Shell.

"She's not his sister," the marshal said, "and you know it. Bass was adopted same as Dorothy Patch. Both of 'em taken in and treated with loving kindness. Old John Patch would cut his own heart out for either of them kids. Only thing was the boy went bad."

"Wait a minute," Shelter said. He placed a hand on the marshal's shoulder as he turned away. Thornhill didn't like it much. His eyes hardened.

"What is it, Morgan?"

"Joe Bass—you talk as if he's a young man."

"He is. Early twenties. Why?"

"Nothing." Shelter shrugged. "There's every chance he's not the man I want then."

"Good. That's one less problem for me," Thornhill said brusquely.

"Another thing, Marshal," Shelter persisted. "You say the kid was brought up by a man named Patch? Why does he call himself Joe Bass then?"

"Simple—or not so simple—simple to the kid's mind. He seems to have done some prowling around in old man

34

Patch's documents box and come up with some evidence that his real father's name was Joe Bass. Since that time he kind of turned bad. He took on his father's name and began making himself trouble of one sort or another around the desert. Now he's topped it—he's gone and kidnapped his own adopted sister and he's holding her ransom. And if I catch the kid now, Morgan, he's going to do some neck dancin'. That's it. If you'll let go of my arm, Morgan? Thanks.

"Boys! Eight o'clock in the morning if the sand's not blowin'. Meet me behind the jail. Two horses if you got 'em, and plenty of grub and water. Joe Bass knows this country like no one but a Tipai knows it. Any man who gets that thousand-dollar reward is going to have earned it. But we'll get him, I promise you that. I promised old John Patch that I'd bring that girl back unharmed, and I mean to keep that promise."

The marshal turned and went out then, the gust of wind blasting fresh sand into the Red Dog. The wind creaked in the trees, hissed softly through the chinks in the stone walls.

Shelter hesitated, looked back at the table he had been sitting at and smiled softly. Clyde was gone, and Shell thought he knew where he had gone. The man had been defensive about this young Joe Bass. Why?

Shelter glanced at the brass-cased clock on the Red Dog's wall. Nearly eight. That gave him twelve hours to get his supplies together, to find another horse, to restock his ammunition.

He was going with the posse. Oh, yes, he was going.

Joe Bass was too young to be Major Joe Bass, CSA, but he was his father's son. Maybe he knew where the old man was. He had taken on the name for some reason. He had begun kicking up his heels for the same reason. Because he wanted to be like Joe Bass? Because Joe Bass, Senior, was running the kid now? A kidnapping—now that wasn't usually a young hothead's crime. Joe Bass? Maybe. Anyway the kid had something to tell and Shelter meant to be there to hear it when he spilled his guts.

That meant riding with the posse, whether Marshal Thornhill liked it or not.

Shell went out into the night. Immediately he was stung on hands, on throat and face by the flying sand. It wasn't thick, but the wind was strong, whining up the street, flapping signs, spinning the old windmill faster and faster, rattling the trees.

Shelter clamped a hand over his hat and headed off toward the general store where a light still showed.

"How are you fixed for .44s?" he asked the storekeeper.

"I've got a crate of 'em, but they're going fast. If I had another half dozen crates I could sell 'em tonight. What's up anyway?"

"A killin' mood," Shell answered. "Let me have what you can and give me two gallon canteens."

Before Shell had gotten out of the general store two more men tramped in out of the sandstorm looking for ammunition. Morgan didn't like them at first sight. Big, red-haired, unshaven, they had a feral gleam in their pale little eyes.

"Be with you in a minute, Sam," the storekeeper called.

"We got us another bounty man here, Sam," the younger, smaller of the redheads said. He leaned against the store counter, tipped back his hat and stood with his feet crossed at the ankles looking at Shell with those pale,

pale eyes.

"Leave be, Hector," the bigger man said gruffly. He was slapping the sand off his clothing vigorously. He wore a duster, torn and frayed at the cufs, nearly new black boots and a pair of Smith & Wesson .36s.

"Get a move on, Herb, will you," he said angrily.

"Yes, Mister Campbell," the storekeeper said with some irony. "You riding out tonight are you?"

"You know I'm not. Shut your face."

"Maybe this fellah is, Sam," Hector Campbell said, still staring at Morgan. He had been drinking and he was primed for trouble. In the morning he was going hunting and the blood lust was surging through him. Shelter recognized it for what it was and he slowly turned away, making it a casual movement, not deliberate enough to offend. They looked for an excuse always, any excuse although they needed none. Perhaps it justified their actions in their own minds.

Shelter was watching the man wrap his packages when the hand fell on his shoulder.

"Are you a big bounty hunting man, Morgan?" Slowly Shell turned to face Hector Campbell. The man was set, his tiny eyes glistening, his lips parted in a humorless grin. "We heard all about you. Heard you're the tough nut. I don't believe it, Morgan. I don't believe a word of it. You gonna have to show me, boy. You drag that Colt out of that holster and show me how mean you are or I'll kill you where you stand."

4.

The store had fallen silent. There was only the hiss of the wind outside, the creaking of a floorboard as big Sam Campbell shifted his feet. Shelter stood looking into the savage little eyes of Hector Campbell, smelling the dirt and whiskey on the man, "Go home and get some rest," Shelter said. "You'll need it in the morning."

"You haven't been paying close attention, Morgan," Hector said, stepping even nearer, his hand locked onto the butt of his Smith & Wesson.

"I've been listening," Shell answered. "Now you do yourself a favor and listen to me." Morgan glanced at big Sam Campbell to see where he stood in this. Hector had a killing urge in him; Sam seemed bored by it, annoyed. But they were brothers and if it came to fighting Sam would back his brother. A glance at the resolute, dull features of Sam Campbell was enough to assure Shelter of that.

"Will you get me some cartridges, damnit, Herb!" Sam Campbell said.

"Uh . . . sure," Herb answered nervously. He looked toward the door of the store, perhaps hoping for help from out of the storm. "Just let me finish with this gentleman . . ."

"This gentleman's finished, Herb," Hector Campbell said. "Aren't you, Morgan? Yes, you're finished. I'll tell you what—if you leave now I'll let you go. If you'll leave on your hands and knees. If you'll crawl to that door and get out of here now I won't bother you. If you don't I'll kill you. Believe it!"

"How much do I owe you?" Shelter asked Herb.

The storekeeper couldn't stammer out an answer for a long minute. "Seven-fifty," he finally managed and Shelter paid him. Shell could feel Hector Campbell at his shoulder, feel his breath on the nape of his neck. Beside Shell was a wooden barrel filled with assorted ax, sledge and mattock handles. When Hector Campbell, in a rage, finally made his move, Shell was ready.

He stepped back, coming up with a curved, hickory ax handle from the barrel. It was a hell of a nice handle, well sanded, the wood selected carefully, and it made a hell of a nice *thunk* on the back of Hector Campbell's skull as he lurched past Shell, trying to draw his precious Smith & Wesson and collar Morgan at the same time.

The ax handle went up quickly, came down hard and Hector Campbell went to the plank floor of the store on his face, smashing his nose against the pine flooring, going out cold.

Shelter hadn't stopped moving. He had struck the blow with his left hand and now his right was filled with the big

39

blue .44. The hammer was back and the gaping barrel was staring right at the head of Sam Campbell.

"What do you say, Sam?"

"Say?" He shrugged. "I don't say nothing when a man has a Colt in my face. Want me to shed my gun?"

"If you would."

He did. Slowly, very carefully. Sam Campbell wasn't a genius, but he was no fool. "Hector will be after you, you know that, don't you?"

"Talk some sense to him, Sam. If he comes after me again I won't let him off with a cracked skull."

"He'll be coming," Sam said with a regretful shake of his head.

"You stop him then."

"Can't do it." Again that almost regretful shake of the big man's head. "Thing is, I'll have to back him. You see how that goes, don't you, Morgan?"

"I see."

"He's my brother, ain't he?"

"Worse luck."

"Yeah—you're telling me. You ready for me, Herb, damnit!" Sam shouted, startling the little man.

When Morgan picked up his goods and left Herb was filling Sam Campbell's order. Hector Campbell was still on the floor, breathing softly, snoring faintly, blood leaking from his nose.

Outside it was dark as sin. Shelter could barely make out the Red Dog across the street or the hotel to the east. He started that way thinking that Joe Bass, Junior was either very lucky or very clever. The sand that was blowing around tonight would cover any sign he had left behind. Shell hoped the men in that posse had a good idea where the kid was heading.

Was he going home? Home to Major Joe Bass, the Carolina butcher? Had he ever even met his father? And how, Shell wondered, was the little girl he had taken away? Dorothy Patch who, although she had lived as brother and sister with Joe Bass, had to be frightened on this night. Taken away from her home out into the desert. Kidnapped by someone she must have trusted. Shelter didn't like this one. He didn't like the taste of it, the smell of it. It wasn't a "natural" crime. A crime of greed or passion—it smacked of the cold-blooded, of vengeance.

The hotel suddenly appeared before Shell and he walked through the screen of dust up the steps and into the lobby, the wind-propelled door banging behind him. A little bald man was at the desk when Shell asked for his room key.

"What time you got, Salty?" Shelter asked.

"Sir?" The little man looked offended.

"Sorry—could you please tell me the time?"

"I have five minutes to eight o'clock, sir," the man said stuffily, slowly and with great dignity examining and replacing his pocket watch.

"Just made it. Thanks."

There was time enough, barely, for Shell to go up to his room, rinse off, slick back his hair and stroll down to the dining room.

He had made a date for that evening, and it wasn't one he was likely to forget.

"May I take your order?" the waiter asked.

"Yes. No menu, thanks. Stuffed pork chops. Two orders. Coffee for two, dessert for two: whatever you've got."

"Fresh peach pie, sir."

"Just the ticket."

"Did you say for two?" the waiter asked in some confusion.

"For two," Morgan replied. Scratching on his pad the waiter walked away. After a while a woman came over and set a second place at the table.

Morgan leaned back, studying the dining room, its handful of inhabitants. An older man in a town suit bent over his plate while his sagging wife incessantly talked at the top of his head, a salesman with his sample bag at his feet, newspaper at his elbow.

Outside it was dark still. The sand beat tiny dancing fingers against the glass of the window panes. Looking up Shelter saw the chandelier, out of place in this western town, unlighted, dusty—maybe there was a story behind it. Indian blankets hung on the opposite wall where cedar planking had been placed over the stone.

"Sir?" The waiter was back, smiling but obviously confused as he laid out a meal for two. The chops were huge, stuffed with cornbread dressing, circled by little potatoes—canned potatoes out here—and a ring of parsley. The coffee was hot. Smoke rose from the barrel of the little silver pot. Both portions of food were set out—the waiter glancing dubiously at Shell as he served to an empty seat. Then he went away and Morgan dug in.

The chops were very good—the meat was well smoked, the dressing southern style made by someone who knew what southern style meant.

It was so good that he nearly started in on the other portion, but there was still time. Still a chance. He poured himself a coffee and sat back; it was then that he saw her.

She came slowly across the room, shy and nervous,

small and womanly, like a doe going to the brook to drink at dawning.

"Is it cold?" she asked.

"I hope not. I'll have them heat it up if it is." Shelter rose and pulled her chair out for her. Merri was wearing a pale blue dress with white lace at the cuffs. Her hair was glossy, neatly pinned, scented softly.

Shelter sat down to sip his coffee, to feast his senses on the woman opposite. From time to time she would lift her eyes shyly and he would smile. Then her cheeks would be touched with pale fire and the eyes would go down again.

"Are you going with the marshal tomorrow?" she asked after the last bite had been swallowed and the waiter had come with two bowls of peach pie and cool cream to pour over it.

"Yes."

"Is it the money?" she asked unexpectedly.

"No. I need to find this man and talk to him. Do you know Joe Bass?"

Merri shook her head. "Not really. Of course I know who he is—everyone knows everyone in Jacumba, but he stays out at the Patch ranch—or did. When his name was Randy Patch, that is. How could you possibly know him, Mister Morgan?"

"I don't. First of all—if you don't call me Shelter, I'm going to get awfully angry with you, remember?" She nodded her head obediently. "I've never met Randy Patch, but I knew a man called Joe Bass. He's the one I'm interested in. A tall, narrow man with almost no flesh on his face. A tight, narrow mouth, small ears, dark, sleek hair brushed straight back. That is Joe Bass—he'd be forty or so now. Do you know him or anyone who looks like that?"

"No," Merri answered simply. There was a bit of pie filling on her upper lip and her pink tongue flicked out to take it off. "Why do you want to find him, may I ask?"

"Something from the old days. The war."

"Is it a long story?"

"Very long. Probably not interesting."

"No? I think it must be," Merri Richardson said. She was toying with her pie now, jabbing at it with the tines of her fork. "You're going to kill him if you find him, aren't you?"

"What makes you say that?"

"You should see your eyes when you talk about him, describe him. Was he awful, Mister . . . Shelter? Was Joe Bass a terrible man?"

"He was scum. Yes, he was awful."

"I'd like to know." She leaned forward and touched his hand, covering it with her own. "I can see you don't care to talk about it, but I'd like to know."

"Would you?" Shell smiled wearily. It was so long ago. So damned far back down the trail. The war. It must have been over ages ago. Everyone else had quit fighting it, but not Shelter Morgan. It was an endless battle, an endless war. He was the endless killer, the hand of retribution.

He tried to tell it briefly, without the blood, without the pain and the terror, the revulsion he felt every time he thought of Georgia, of the last days of a bloody war.

"It was in the last days, Merri. Down along the Conasauga River in Georgia. There wasn't much left of us. A few rags holding men together as the winter settled in. My God, some of my people were barefoot and there was snow on the ground. We fought on because that was our duty. We fought on and we froze and we went hungry and

44

some of us died in pain because there wasn't any medicine.

"That was why when they gave me the chance, I leaped at it."

"What chance, Shelter?"

"You've heard of Chickamauga? Yes, there was a terrible battle there. We lost—we, the South—we got kicked and shoved and run out of there. During the battle a man named General Custis had hidden some Confederate property near Lookout Mountain, Tennessee. It was still supposedly there and they wanted a volunteer to go after it."

"Property?"

Shell lifted his eyes. "Gold, Merri. A quarter of a million dollars in gold. That was what Custis had hidden at Lookout—and now Lookout was behind enemy lines."

"Why you?" she asked.

"I was born near there. I'm a Tennessee boy. My home is actually in Pikeville—that's only a stone's throw from Lookout . . ." for a moment Shelter appeared wistful, perhaps thinking of home. He had been there once since the war. Once only and even there they had tried to kill him. The gold had gotten into their blood as well.

"So you went?"

"I went. I knew the backtrails, the high ridges, the bottoms. I went, taking four handpicked men with me. Men who trusted me, whom I trusted. The best of the best."

"But you didn't find the gold?"

"Did I say that?" Shell shook his head. "I guess I wish I hadn't found it. That the Yankees had taken it off to their king in Washington. But we found it, yes, with a little luck, and we got it the hell out of there. I lost one man who was told to keep his head down and didn't, but we recovered the gold which was to be used for medical supplies, for food and blankets, for shoes, all of which could have been had through British blockade runners— or so they had convinced me.

"We needed those goods, needed them badly. There were thousands of us starving and come spring there would be only a few hundred. I knew that. They were freezing to death around me. There were soldiers who were going to have their feet amputated from the frost-bite they got marching barefoot through the snow to fight. That's how bad it was—I can't describe it if you weren't there. They screamed at night and there was no morphine to hammer down the pain in them. That was what I wanted the gold for!" Shell's hand slammed down against the table. The drummer across the way glanced at him in annoyance. "That was what they said it was going to be used for—my superior officers who sent me on that mission."

The bitterness was seeping out now and Merri gave it time to cool before she asked.

"What did happen to the gold?"

"It was used to line the pockets of a few traitors, a few cowards, men who had been given the privilege of command. It never got to where it was going and as a result hundreds—hundreds—of men died that winter, in horrible pain, bellies shriveling, slowly freezing . . ."

"What happened?" Merri pushed away her dessert. It was impossible to enjoy it.

"The four of us who were left escorted the gold back to Georgia, back toward the bloody, bloody Conasauga where General Curtis was to meet us. We were elated— the four of us. We had beaten some long odds making it in and out of the Yankee lines. Carrying that gold it was chancy, very chancy. But we had made it.

"A courier rode out to meet us and he led us to where General Custis and Colonel Fainer, my commanding officer—my friend—waited. They weren't alone.

"There were something over twenty men waiting there in that clearing among the shell-blackened oaks. Officers and men, all of them in civilian clothes."

"You knew what they wanted."

"Sure. We knew right away. They tried to talk at first—about the war, how it was lost and everyone knew it. How we ought to take what we could and get the hell out."

"Joe Bass . . ."

"Yes, Major Joe Bass. I recall his line perfectly. The Confederacy owed us something. We'd fought for nearly five years, mostly without pay. At the end of the war the Yankees were going to take our property, our women, likely imprison all of us.

"He sat a black horse, dressed in a gray suit with a narrow tie. Hatless. The wind lifted his straight dark hair. That face of his was set—I've never seen a face with the skin so taut, stretched over the cheekbones as if there was no flesh at all beneath it.

"They were talking like that," Shelter went on, "and suddenly we weren't talking. The guns were firing, men were falling. When it was over they had the gold and I was the only one left behind to tell about it. I was on the run north, but I wasn't going good—they had gotten lead into me. Wouldn't you know it?" Shelter smiled ironically. "I ran smack into a Yankee patrol. They saved my life. And then arrested me."

"Arrested?"

"Sure. I was wearing civilian clothes. They arrested me for a spy and locked me up. I got seven years, Merri.

Seven long years while those who had taken the gold fled the South, most of them coming West to live. Many of them using new names. They lived high, I guess. While other, better men, lay dead in the Georgia earth. And I sat and I made my vows that they wouldn't get away with it."

"Why didn't you go to the authorities?" Merri asked with touching ingenuousness.

"I did. I went to the Justice Department—after I came out of prison, after the war had long been over, the thieves scattered to the winds. They just weren't interested. I was told that it was probably impossible to find all of them, that the entire West couldn't be combed for a crime I alleged had been commited. If they had been found, if the government had put years of effort and thousands of dollars into the job, well, I was told, there still wasn't any legal case against them. It was my word against theirs, and that just doesn't carry the weight to convict anyone of anything."

"So you took things into your own hands?"

"That's right." Shelter's lips compressed into a straight line. "I took it into my own hands."

"And that's why you want Joe Bass. Only he's not *the* Joe Bass. It's a little confusing."

"Isn't it? But if I can find Joe Bass and keep the posse from killing him . . ."

"Killing him!"

"Yes, ma'am. That poster read 'dead or alive', and dead is a whole lot easier. I've ridden with some posses and lady, you ought to see those guns come up when they spot the man they're after—whoever kills the outlaw, you see, is awarded the prize. They shoot fast under those circumstances."

"Yes . . . I guess they would."

"That doesn't bother you too much does it?" Shell

48

lifted her chin with his index finger. "You hardly know Joe Bass, after all."

"That's right. I hardly know him. But I don't like to see anyone hurt, anything killed."

"No. I don't either."

"Not you, Shelter. I don't want to see you killed."

"I won't be."

"You're pretty sure of yourself."

Yes. He was pretty sure of himself because he had to be. If you stopped and thought about it you weren't any good at it any longer. And he had to keep at it—there was a list of names in Shelter's pocket. A lot of those names had had a red line drawn through them, but there were still a lot to go. Men like Major Bass. Men who had to pay for what they had done before Morgan could ever quit. He had made his vows; he had promised the dead.

"Are you going to eat that pie?" Shell asked. His voice had changed. He had relaxed, and instead of being the hunter, he was temporarily a quite handsome, nearly boyish male.

Merri laughed, and it was a nice laugh, musical, cheerful. Then she saw that Morgan was looking into her eyes in a way that wasn't funny at all. It was frightening and thrilling at once.

"I never . . ." she began, but he interrupted her.

"Then don't." Shelter held up a hand. "And for God's sake, don't apologize. I hate it when people apologize for nothing. Finish your coffee and let's talk about something else."

"And after that?"

"After that I'm going to my room. I'm going to turn off the lamp and crawl in bed. I'm not going to lock the door behind me."

5.

Shelter stood naked in his room looking out the window. The storm seemed to be abating. The wind which had been rattling the trees outside now whispered gentle secrets. The air was clearer. Here and there a star had managed to break through the dust clouds. Jacumba was locked up, silent but for the Red Dog Saloon where the men were priming themselves for the adventure to come.

At the tap on the door Shelter turned slowly. "Come in," he said and the door opened slowly. Merri stood there backlighted by a distant lantern burning up the hall. She stood there for a moment and then came in, walking softly as if she was on quicksand and afraid of being swallowed up.

Shelter was standing there naked and she seemed surprised but hardly shocked. The door closed behind Merri and there was only the light of the clouded sky falling through the hotel window.

"I didn't think I'd come," Merri said.

"I'm glad you did."

"I didn't even think I'd show up at dinner. Shelter—what are you doing to me? All sorts of things I don't want to do you make me do."

"I won't make you do anything, Merri. You can leave now if you want."

"I don't want—that's it, don't you see?" She came forward very quickly and was against Shelter, clinging to him, her lips touching his bare shoulder and then drawing away.

"Undress me," she said.

It was a pleasure. Shell worked at the hooks and buttons, slowly drawing the dress from her shoulders, pausing to kiss neck and shoulders, the slender back along the spine. He turned her, slipped the dress down to her waist and let it slide to the floor in a wreath, the fabric whispering softly as it fell.

Shelter stood before her, tilting her head back. He kissed her deeply, feeling her soft lips part, tense, search hungrily, her hands go to his shoulders and grip him tightly.

"The rest of my clothes," Merri said and Shelter nodded. He unfastened her chemise and let it join the dress on the floor. The white undergarment fell free and her full, rosebud tipped breasts bobbed free to dazzle Shell's admiring eyes. His hands slid up, cupping them as his head lowered, his lips searching the nipples, finding them taut and swollen.

"Shell . . ." She gasped something, something not quite a complaint, not quite encouragement. Then she

51

sagged against him, kicking free of the rest of her clothing as they went to his bed, the springs giving forth an outrageous squeak as Merri rolled onto her back, her eyes sparkling in the darkness, her lips parted, her hands reaching behind Shelter, gripping his hard-muscled buttocks, sliding between his legs to encircle his shaft, to heft his sack. And she sighed again.

"Shell," she said and this time it was encouragement, all encouragement.

Morgan didn't need much. He was on hands and knees, his lips exploring her body, traversing breasts and shoulders, working down across the soft expanse of her belly, trekking along the smooth length of her inner thighs, her scent ripe and intriguing in his nostrils as Merri reached for him from behind, her hands clinging to his erection, toying with it, gripping tightly until he turned to find her, legs spread, breast rising and falling as with exertion, needing him.

He crept forward and her thighs spread, her knees uplifted. She had his shaft still and she guided him home, touching him to her warm inner flesh with a slight shudder. Slowly she worked him forward, breathing intently. A fraction of an inch at a time she took him, wanting him to fill her deeply, holding back as her fingers searched Shelter, as she touched herself.

Her legs had slowly raised until they were straight up in the air. Still Merri held Shelter, her other hand reaching behind him to cup his sack, to grope for him as Shelter began to sway against her, to dip and rock in her dampness.

Merri's feet lowered and her heels pressed against Shelter's buttocks, urging him on, delivering a cadenced message as he hovered over her and then buried himself

52

to the hilt, feeling Merri shudder and sway beneath him.

Merri's head had begun to roll slowly from side to side. Her hands were everywhere, probing, touching, grappling. She took his head between her hands and drew his mouth to her own, kissing him deeply as her hips continued their steady movement, her pelvis grinding against Shell's.

She panted into his mouth, her body was growing slick with the sheen of perspiration. Her hair was damp at the ends as she worked against him with steady intensity until suddenly she arched her back, groaned, ground her teeth against Shell's lips and came completely undone, finishing with a slow series of urgent thrusts.

By then Shelter was ready, past ready and he gripped the back of her neck, holding her kiss. His other hand slipped beneath her ass and lifted her as he drove it home time and again, the scent of her, the heat of her body, the deep-throated moaning lifting him to a sudden hard climax which drained him, left Merri panting, satisfied and filled with liquid warmth.

She wasn't there when he awoke. The room was dark but there was a grayness to the eastern skies which meant that dawn wasn't far off.

He sat up rubbing the back of his neck. He saw the dark silk stocking on the floor nearly beneath his feet and he smiled distantly.

Shell rose and padded naked across the room to look out the window. A light breeze seemed to be stirring but the sand wasn't moving. The posse would be leaving at eight o'clock and he was going with them.

He dressed, walked downstairs and ate breakfast, his eyes searching the corridor, the doorways, the desk, looking for Merri—but she was nowhere to be seen.

Embarrassed? He hoped not, she certainly had nothing to be embarrassed about.

Shelter ate slowly, hoping she might show up, but no such luck. He finished the eggs, ham, biscuits and three cups of coffee and went back upstairs.

The door to his room was open but Merri was not there—the stocking, however, was gone.

Shell shrugged and packed his roll. The dawn light was on the window, making a reddish-blue smear of it. A patch of clear yellow was marked on the wooden floor. A mockingbird sang outside not far away. The desert beyond already looked hot and dry and it undoubtedly was. Shell made a mental note to fill those canteens of his to the cap.

Downstairs he clomped, still looking for Merri, not finding her. He paid the little bald man at the desk and then hung around the lobby for a while, waiting.

It was no use. She didn't show and there was nothing more to be done. Shelter went out into the crisp sunlight of new morning and stretched his arms, inhaling deeply. Then he headed off toward the livery stable across town, finding it a busy place on this morning.

"Yes, sir, yes sir?" a quick little man in a straw hat said by way of greeting.

"Got a saddle horse for sale?"

"Yes, sir, I do. And I wish I had a dozen more this morning. I'd get top dollar for all of them. I'm asking top dollar for these." He walked Shelter along past a row of stalls where other buyers, other posse members were examining hoof and fetlock, teeth and wind. "Not that I'm cheating anyone, you see." Shelter nodded. "But when there's demand the price goes up, doesn't it?"

"It seems to."

"This buckskin," the stableman said, "I can let you have for a hundred—"

"Show me a horse," Morgan said.

"Yes?" The man's eyebrow lifted and lurking cupidity flashed for a moment in those brown eyes. "You're willing to pay are you?"

"I'm willing to pay the regular price for the best horse you've got. The regular price, you understand? Not this morning's price. You make the decision. Sell to me or wait for someone else with the cash money." And Morgan figured that would be a long wait in a town like Jacumba.

"Ain't this John Peters' old sorrel?" someone yelled from across the stable. The man in the straw hat didn't pay any attention. His eyes were fixed on Morgan, measuring, weighing the alternatives.

"Come on," the stableman said. "Out back."

They went out into the fenced yard. There were three horses tethered there. Two a pair of matched blacks, someone's fancy buggy team; the other was a short-coupled, white-blazed roan with a fiery eye and quick feet which it stamped now as the two men approached.

"You look that over," the stableman said. "If you want him you come in and give me a hundred and fifty dollars cash money—no dickering."

With that the man went back inside and Shelter moved to the roan, running a hand along its sleek, muscular flank. Beneath the hide, muscle twitched. The roan's ears were up, alert and intent. Yet it wasn't a nervous animal, only quick and still a little young—under three years old, Morgan thought—but it would be a horse. It definitely would be.

He didn't dicker. His boot money was considerably

55

diminished when he rode toward the marshal's office half an hour later, but Morgan was well mounted on the feisty little roan, leading the gray which was more horse but which was still run down from the trek across the foothills and would be better off travelling light for a time.

There were thirty men in back of the marshal's office—smoking, shouting, joking, some of them drinking already, others just hung over.

Hector Campbell stood next to his brother in a small knot of five men across the yard. His eyes met Shell's but there was nothing in them. There was plenty going on in that tiny brain, Shell imagined, only now wasn't the time for it. Even Hector Campbell wasn't that stupid.

Shelter swung down, waited to water his horses at the marshal's trough and glanced around, measuring his fellow hunters. There wasn't much to them for the most part. Townsmen out for a little excitement, a day or two away from the wife, a chance at the thousand dollars.

The Campbells, however, were at the center of a cadre of much harder looking men. There were seven or eight of them now. They were well-armed, well-provisioned and looked like they meant business. There were eyes following Shell wherever he moved. He ignored it and settled in to wait.

He didn't have long.

At quarter to eight Marshal Jeb Thornhill came out of the back door of his jail, a blanket roll over his shoulder, Winchester in hand. Behind him was a stalky deputy who apparently was going to stay behind and hold things down.

"Mornin'," Thornhill said crisply. He looked around for a moment, his eyes pausing longest on Shelter Morgan. "If you're ready, men, let's ride. First stop is the

Patch place. I want to talk to old John before we go looking for his kid."

In less than a minute everyone was aboard the horses. The animals milled, nickered, stamped their feet and blew through their nostrils as the marshal saddled and swung up himself, ready to lead them out.

"Let's get going," Thornhill said and he waved his arm. There was a little uneasiness in the marshal's manner, Shell thought. Maybe the marshal had seen mobs before too, and that was what Morgan thought he was seeing here—an embryonic mob looking for a catalyst, a target to be torn to bits.

No one else was eager to apparently, so Shell rode ahead to side the marshal as they rode out of the south end of town through a long, arid valley ringed by hills which lacked any semblance of soil and appeared to be, and were, only stacks of boulders.

The sun was hot already. A rivulet of sweat raced down the marshal's cheek.

"You just had to come along, did you?" Thornhill said gruffly.

"Yes. That's it; I had to."

"I hear you ran into Hector Campbell last night."

"Word gets around fast in this town, doesn't it?"

"You watch yourself. Hector's a mean boy."

"Is he?"

"Tough, aren't you?" the sheriff said sourly.

"Sometimes, yeah. Looking at what you've got behind you here, Marshal, I'd say you could use at least one tough man."

"There's some that are pretty tough—" the marshal shifted half around, his saddle creaking. "That maverick with the long black mustache is Jack Claypool. By rights

57

he should have had his neck stretched long ago. But I've got nothing on him, like I've nothing hard on you, Morgan."

"Doesn't it strike you funny that Claypool, and the Campbells would want to ride out with the posse?"

"Why?" A thousand dollars will draw all kinds. Hell, that's nearly three years' wages, ain't it? It brought you, didn't it, Morgan?"

"No, not me. I'm not along for the money."

"Oh, that's right—you just want to talk to Joe Bass," the marshal said caustically.

"That's all. I want to talk to him about his father."

"A thousand doesn't mean a thing to you." The marshal turned his head and spat. Dangerous in the breeze.

"I could use a thousand, sure," Morgan said, "but I do all right without money when I don't have it. I don't mean to argue with anybody over rights to it." He glanced back at the rest of the posse. "Besides, none of us has even seen Joe Bass yet, have we?"

"No," Thornhill said, "but we will, Morgan. We will— I promise you that. They want the thousand, those people back there. Patch, he wants his daughter back. Me—I've got a job I like pretty well, know what I mean? I want to protect that job. I can't have every crazy kid in the country pulling stuff like this. Uh-uh, not in my territory."

They rode silently on. The grass had begun to green a little though it was still sparse and short. Here and there Morgan saw old gnarled live oaks and a cottonwood or two. The trail had widened a little and there were wagon ruts carved into it. They rode around a bend overlooked

58

by a huge towerlike stack of boulders and were suddenly there.

Below was a deeply carved, deep green valley where cattle grazed. A silver-blue ribbon wound its way across the little valley, past the white house beyond. A white house with a green roof, a barn painted similarly, white fences. It was quite a place Joe Bass Junior had turned his back on.

"What makes a kid do that?" Morgan wondered out loud.

"Do what? Turn bad?"

"That's right. Did he have a grudge against Patch?"

"Not that anyone ever heard of."

"Doesn't make sense."

"I don't know. He found out that he wasn't who he thought he was and it shocked him. He was an outlaw's son and he was determined to become one."

"Maybe. You're going to talk to the old man—mind if I listen in?"

"He's not well," Marshal Thornhill said. They rode through the deep grass now, the cattle moving slowly away from them, sleek and fat in the sunlight. "I don't suppose it will hurt anything for you to come in, but I don't see the real need for it."

"I just want to hear what he has to say."

"All right." Thornhill shrugged. "Just don't do anything to upset the old man.

"I don't intend to," Morgan answered. Thornhill stared at him for a minute, grunted, spat and looked away again.

The house was well kept up but there was a look of incipient decay about it, something Morgan couldn't quite define. The house, the land seemed diseased, on the verge of collapse. Maybe Joe Bass had ridden off with whatever vigor the place had had.

A Mexican kid held their horses while they went in. There were three of them. The marshal, the bank's vice-president, a smooth man named Richard Yeats, and Morgan. Shell wondered how the bank could spare Yeats and what that sort of a man wanted to go riding on the desert for, but then perhaps Yeats was wondering the same thing about him.

The house was spacious, cool although it was nearing ninety outside. There were white curtains on the small windows—a woman's work, a white tablecloth on the big table in the dining room. In the den beyond a collapsed remnant of a man sat in a big leather chair staring at an empty fireplace.

The marshal took off his hat and with a glance at the other two men stepped around in front of John Patch. Shelter could see Patch in profile and what he saw was not healthy. The man was broken. He must have run to near three hundred pounds. His fingers were heavy and white. His neck sagged in great folds. His jowels drooped in his jawline. On his lap was a tinted photograph, a photograph of a young and very beautiful, blond haired girl.

"I don't understand the world, Jeb," John Patch said. One of his pudgy hands lifted and wiped back the mass of snowy hair on his head. When the hand lowered again it rested on the picture. "I just don't understand. I raised that boy right. Nursed him when he was ill, bought him his first pony . . . you got to find that boy, Jeb. You got to find Dorothy."

"Sure, John. Have you heard from the boy?"

"No." The great bulldog head shook from side to side. "Just that first note. Five thousand dollars or he says he'll kill her. His own sister!" The voice rose to a rumble. For a moment power seemed to gather in that huge flaccid form, to brace the shoulders and chest. Then it drifted away and John Patch was left puddled in his chair.

"I withdrew the money from your account, Mister Patch," the banker said. "You'll have to sign the authorization here."

Shelter glanced at Yeats, understanding now why the vice president of the Jacumba bank was along. He was carrying the ransom money. Five thousand dollars worth. Shelter wondered if anyone else in the posse knew about this.

A pen had to be placed in John Patch's hand. Yeats supported the paper while the old man signed it.

"May I ask you something, sir?" Shelter stepped forward and the eyes of John Patch slowly shifted to Morgan, narrowing, questioning.

"Do I know you?"

"No, sir. My name's Shelter Morgan. I wanted to know what you could tell me about Joe Bass."

"Joe Bass." The old man's head sagged as if he had thought so long about Joe Bass that there was nothing left to do but suffer. "I can't tell you anything."

"He's your son's real father."

"I can't tell you anything. I won't, unless . . ." Patch glanced at the marshal.

"He's not a lawman, John. You don't have to answer."

"Mister Patch, this could be important to you and to me. Where did you find the boy? How did you come to adopt him? Is his father alive or dead?"

"I don't know. I don't know," John Patch said, his

great head slowly wagging from side to side. A tear broke free from his eyes and fell, dropping onto the photograph on his lap. The marshal looked at Shell and shook his head meaningfully.

"We'll find her, John. I swear it to you."

"He's gone mad. The boy's gone mad." A thick white hand shot out suddenly and gripped the marshal's wrist. "You get her! You get my Dorothy back. To hell with the money! That money don't mean a damn thing to me without my little girl. If you have to pay him, you pay him." His voice lowered to a tight little hiss. "If you have to kill him, you kill him, Jeb, because he's gone bad. He's got his father's blood and he's gone bad. You get my Dorothy, Jeb Thornhill. You get her and don't bring me any excuse. You bring her to me if you have to ride over dead men and horses to do it, if you have to ride into the bloody maw of hell! You bring her!"

6.

Jeb Thornhill knew what to do, thank God. John Patch had worked himself up into a frenzy. His blubbery face had gone fiery red and then dead white as he boomed out his orders at the marshal.

Finally he just collapsed in his chair and Thornhill walked hurriedly to a little table near the door, calling out for someone as he scrabbled around in the table drawer, coming up with a bottle of smelling salts and some little yellow pills.

"Theresa! Theresa!" The marshal boomed and after a minute they heard the scurrying footsteps on the tiled corridor and a stout Mexican woman arrived, her skirts hoisted as she rushed to the ranch owner.

"How is he?" Yeats asked.

"He's coming around already," Thornhill said. To Morgan, John Patch didn't look good at all. His flesh was gray. Purple and blue veins ran in a network of tangled threads across cheeks and nose. His eyes fluttered open and stared without recognition at the people gathered around him.

"I think he be all right," Theresa said. Then, more sharply, "I think he be better off if you all go right now. No more talk about the boy, about Dorothy, I think. Go now, go on, please!"

"She's right," Thornhill said planting his hat. He looked as if he was going to say something else to John Patch but he didn't. Patch likely wouldn't have heard or understood anyway. The big man was right on the edge. Heart attack, collapse weren't but a step or two away. They crept out quietly, hearing Theresa tell one of the white-clad Mexican boys to ride for the doctor.

The white glare outside, the heat seemed doubly intense after the cool darkness of the house. Shelter swung aboard the roan and sat waiting while the marshal and Yeats had a short private conference. It was about the ransom money, had to be. Shelter, glancing casually around saw other eyes on the marshal. Those of the Campbells and the coal black eyes of the mustached gunman, Jack Claypool.

"Those three," Shelter told himself, "mean to get paid for this one way or the other."

The marshal spent another fifteen minutes talking to an old Indian who worked on the ranch and who had seen Joe Bass snatch the girl and make his escape.

"That way. He go that way. That way. Onto desert, toward big hole."

"And he was alone, Manta?" the marshal asked.

"Alone then, yes, but not alone all the time."

"What do you mean?"

"Manta hear other horses. Beyond the trees other horses call to this horse. Maybe four, five horses?" The old Indian rubbed his arm and shrugged.

"He headed for the flats though. You're sure? He didn't circle back toward the hills?"

"No. Flats. Manta followed. I don't run good now. Too damned old, you know? Saw much dust though, much dust out on desert and that day there was no wind."

"All right. You know the kid, Manta. Where was he heading?"

Shelter who was watching, listening without appearing to, thought he detected hesitation in the old Indian's eyes. Manta told the marshal, "Don't know. Big desert, big place. That boy he knows it all. Knows plenty of places."

"No place special? Maybe someplace with water that Manta showed him?"

"He knows plenty of places," the Indian repeated.

"All right." The marshal turned away. "Any of you *hombres* hasn't filled his canteens better do so right now. I've got no idea where this trail's leading, but I'll guarantee it's going to be dry."

Incredibly there were a few men who hadn't filled their canteens. The rest of the posse waited as these swung down and filled up at the well, lowering the canteens on a slender length of line.

"You want to go with us, Manta?" the marshal asked. "Maybe track for us. I'll give you five dollars a day."

"Maybe too old. Manta is too old," the Indian answered. He looked old, maybe, but he was all wire and leather that one, and Shell would have bet he could have run any of them into the ground on a long trek. "They need me here I bet. Boss needs me here. Old boss is sick."

65

"All right," Thornhill said, getting the idea. "That's it then. It's a huge area, men. If the kid had sense enough to ride while the sand was blowing and to stop when the sand stopped, we'll never find him. I'm hoping his hideout, wherever it is, is more than a day's ride out, that he's still riding now. That way we've some hope of eventually cutting sign.

"If we see them at range don't anyone start firing. You accidentally hit the girl and you'll hang, I promise you. This is my last bit of advice—this is going to be a son of a bitch. It's bad out there, very bad this time of the year. Anybody that is beginning to have doubts, do me a favor. Do yourself a favor and pull off. Go back to town and have yourself a cool one."

No one pulled off. It was a mistake. They should have listened—it would have kept a few more men alive.

They rode out raising a dust cloud that must have been visible for mile upon mile. The bounty killers, two dozen strong wanting money and blood. What made them any different from the kid they were hunting? Maybe they weren't as good. Nobody had said a word about Randy Patch having killed anyone.

Shelter was tired of the marshal's conversation. He let the mob go past him, then riding slightly off to the west to avoid the dust, he trailed after them. He never had liked having that many guns at his back.

They funneled through a narrow rocky valley farther south and the posse slowed as the trail became a path picked over ruts and rocks in the dry, whitish earth. There was a considerable grade now. The trail to the desert flats wound down through the barren canyon. The wind that reached them now was dry, very dry, superheated as air was forced up the wedge-shaped canyon.

66

Far distant was a stretch of chocolate colored foothills seen through a wavering haze. A distant blue mirage glittered against the white flats, cool, soft-appearing.

"Think we'll catch him by nightfall?"

The kid had eased up beside Shelter. He had let him come. He looked harmless, green as a willow branch . . . but then there were a lot of harmless looking kids with big guns who liked nothing better than to split your brisket for you.

"I don't think we're likely to have that much luck," Shell responded.

"No?" The kid worked his paint pony over the rough ground. They could see the rest of the posse ahead, snaking down toward the desert. "I was kind of hoping it would be a quick chase. Mara Lee . . . well, I've got a girl I was going to see tonight and if I don't I guess someone else might."

"You should have turned back when the marshal gave you the chance."

"Maybe." The kid shrugged narrow shoulders and grinned. "I guess I would have but I didn't want everyone to think I was scared or something."

"It really doesn't matter what people think," Morgan said. The kid shrugged. A wisp of straw colored hair stuck out from beneath his hat, curling across his forehead.

"It does, you know," he replied. "Maybe not to you—I don't know. But to me it matters. I live in the same town with these people. I will for a hell of a long time . . ." his eyes lifted to the desert. "Not tonight, huh?"

"Not tonight."

Maybe not tomorrow, maybe not next week or next month. Shelter was settled in for a long hunt. However things came out he meant to find Randy Patch—or Joe

Bass as he called himself—and have a good long talk with him.

"Did you know the man?" Shell asked.

"Randy? Sure. We used to hunt together, and we washed dishes at the hotel one summer for a little cash. Then his old man . . . Mr. Patch, that is, took us on one spring for a drive down to San Diego. Yes, I know Randy Patch about as well as anyone."

And that didn't seem to be saying much. No one apparently knew the kid very well, how his mind was working.

"Did he ever come to you after he changed his name?"

"No."

"To explain what was going on."

"I never saw him. Nobody knows what happened. Nobody but Randy . . . Joe Bass."

The kid's name was Dave Becker. He talked a little too much but Shell didn't mind his company. It was better companionship than some of the others on that trail would offer. Like Hector Campbell.

"He's killed men," Dave said, his voice lowering to a whisper although the Campbells were far ahead of them, perhaps half a mile as the posse reached the alkali flats and stretched out eastward.

"Has he?"

"Sure. The marshal knows it, but they never had any evidence."

"There seldom is," Shell answered. Not out here. You had to kill a man in the center of town at high noon to even be noticed. What went on up in the foothills when two men were alone no one knew.

"Him and his brother both," Dave Becker persisted.

"And Jack Claypool—why he must have killed half a dozen!"

"Do tell." Shelter's eyes were on the distances, squinting into the hard glare rising off the flats. White dust rose from the horses' hoofs and quickly dissipated. The sun lay across unprotected flesh like a branding iron. You couldn't touch the metal on a horse's bridle without burning fingers.

"Where's the marshal heading?" Shell wondered out loud.

"I don't know. I don't know this country."

"No? The marshal seems to. He's got a definite idea where we're going. I believe I'll have a little chat with him."

The chance for that came sooner than expected. Coming up over a chalky hillrise they found a green pool no more than twenty feet across, fifty long. There the marshal reined up and swung down, loosening his cinch, slipping the bit from his buckskin horse's mouth.

"Last chance for water, men. Get those horses' bellies filled. Me, I'm changing horses as well. It's best to alternate—one animal for morning, one for afternoon. Do what you want, but get some water in them. If there's water for fifty miles after this I don't know where the hell it is."

"Where are we heading, marshal?" Shelter Morgan asked.

"East."

"Come on, let's be friendly."

"I've tried to be, Morgan," the marshal answered, removing his hat to pat at his forehead with a folded red kerchief. "Even though you smell like trouble to me."

69

"You going to answer me or preach to me?" Shell was rubbing the roan's back. He spoke without looking at the marshal who was on the far side of the horse.

"The hills," Thornhill said tersely. "A man can't hole up on the desert, can he? Even if he has water he can't fort up. There's nothing to get behind, no place to hide."

"Your reasoning sounds all right."

The marshal was looking at the distant hills, dark and serrated against the pale blue skyline. "It's my best guess, that's all. I got to do something, don't I Morgan?"

"Sure, you've got to do something."

"I can't just sit there."

"No—besides, I reckon the ransom note said to bring the money out to the hills, didn't it?" Shell asked casually.

"How in the flaming hell . . . !" the marshal exploded. "Who told you about that? Yeats? I'll twist his neck for him."

"It was only a guess, Thornhill."

"A guess?"

"That's right. I know you've got the ransom money, five thousand dollars. I know when folks ask for ransom they most often tell where they want it delivered. Also, you're heading straight as a bee toward those hills."

"Who have you told about this?" The marshal was anxious, damned anxious.

"No one. But they know," Shell said, smoothing the saddle blanket on the big gray's back, throwing the saddle up in one easy motion.

"How do you know?"

"Their eyes. They can't keep them from Yeats and his saddlebags. The Campbells and Jack Claypool—a couple of those other hard cases with them. You think they came out to rescue the girl, do you? Because they have an interest in justice?"

"The reward . . ."

"The reward's a long shot and they know it. The gold Yeats has," Shelter said with a wink, "now that's a sure thing."

"I can't buy it. To grab that reward money they'd have to kill me and they know it."

"Yeah." Shell's voice was flat. He kneed the gray, strapped the double cinches down and nodded to the marshal.

"With all these people around!"

"Maybe we won't be all that many when it happens, Marshal Thornhill."

"If you're trying to scare me, I don't scare easy."

"No, I didn't think you did. But you've got reason to be scared now, out here where anything can happen and only those who make it back can say what happened. I'd watch myself, were I you, marshal, I surely would. Those are some hard men there and they didn't come riding for their health. Nor for yours."

The day dragged past them, an endless white blur, dust-choked, blistering. Shelter shifted in the saddle from time to time and even that was an effort as the day dragged past. Nothing grew out on the Anza-Borrego as they called the desert. Nothing but long, whiplike ocotillo with flowering red tips, nothing but occasional greasewood or jumping cholla cactus. Now and then something quick and deadly could be seen moving among the rocks, a pale, pale sidewinder, its hooded eyes watching intently, the waddling clumsy form of a deadly gila monster.

And above, the vultures which seemed to know, somehow seemed to know. They waited with eternal patience. They would be fed in time. Death was a constant on the desert.

They made dry camp at the edge of a cracked and sere wadi. Among the dark, volcanic rocks they built a fire and got to boiling coffee. Shelter watched them gloomily. It was a damned swell picnic they were having. That fire was visible for twenty miles.

Shell took care of his horses, hobbling them side by side in a nook in the abrupt, shallow canyon below the rocks. There flash floods had rampaged in the past, but there would be no rain in the mountains on this night. The stars were a milky blur across the velvet sky. Distantly a coyote called and was answered. Shelter walked back to the fire, studying the faces there, the townsmen and the marshal, and across from them the hard men. Campbell's crowd. The two brothers, the lanky, slow talking Jack Claypool and two others—one of them an Indian, one a beefy looking bald man with a bad scar across one eye from hairline to jaw.

"Evenin'," Shelter said to the marshal as he hunkered down next to the fire with his tin cup in hand. The marshal felt disinclined to answer. Shell grinned and picked up the folded towel which lay on the rock near the fire. With that he picked up the coffee pot which was nestled in the coals.

He poured himself a cup of coffee but he never got it to his lips.

The thin shower of sand was kicked through the fire to spray itself onto Shell, into his cup. Morgan just crouched there for a minute, lips pursed. He glanced up and saw the dull little eyes of Hector Campbell looking back. Gleeful little pig eyes.

Shell sighed, dumped out his cup of coffee and tried again. He refilled his cup and again Hector kicked up the sand. Again the sand spattered Shell, sprayed into his coffee cup.

Hector was still grinning—he had that kind of a mind.

He was so pleased with himself that he wasn't ready for it, not at all ready when Shell's hand swept down and drew that big Colt from his belt holster. The click of the hammer being drawn back was loud in the silence which had fallen over the camp.

"Morgan!" the marshal shouted.

"Butt out, Thornhill," Morgan said coldly.

"I won't have this, Morgan."

Shell didn't bother answering him. His eyes, the barrel of that Colt were trained on Hector Campbell who was still smiling. A little weakly now, however, a little crookedly.

"Pour me a cup of coffee, Hector. Please?" Shell's voice was soft, but there was something in it that a more experienced man would have paid some attention to. Something menacing, too confident.

"You got to hell, Morgan, you lousy son of a bitch . . ." the rest of it was cut off by the report of the .44. Hector screamed with pain and clapped a hand to his ear. Blood leaked through the fingers. Campbell leaped to his feet, howling. Sam Campbell started to move but Shell's sights had already switched that way.

"It's not worth it, Sam. Not for a little bit of ear."

"Damn you! Damn you!" Hector Campbell repeated monotonously.

He had taken his hand away now and despite the blood they could see that the lobe of his right ear was missing. Someone whistled in admiration. The man could shoot.

"Morgan!" Thornhill said loudly. "I won't have this. Put that gun away, do you hear? No more trouble."

It was too late to stop the trouble. Shelter holstered his gun, and that might have been the end of it, except that Hector Campbell had to get even, he had to have his back. He made his play as Shelter's Colt touched the bottom of the holster.

"Look out," Dave Becker screamed, but it was already too late for a warning.

7.

Shelter holstered his Colt and turned a quarter away. It was a quarter too much. He heard the savage bellow and glanced back in time to see Hector Campbell hurl himself through the campfire and collide with Morgan.

They went down together, Hector's big fist glancing off Shell's jaw, starting the bells to ringing, lighting up a dark corner of his brain. Shell got a forearm up and drove it against Campbell's windpipe, driving him back for a second, long enough for the fuzziness to clear away.

Shell tried to get to his feet, but Campbell was up first and as Shell rose to one knee Campbell kicked out savagely, his bootheel just grazing Shelter's temple as he yanked away from the kick. If it had landed it would have caved in Shell's skull for him. Campbell was a big man and he had all of his force behind it.

In the background Shell was dimly aware of voices

shouting, of faces firelit and excited. "Kill him," someone repeated half a dozen times. No one was shouting for them to stop it.

It wasn't going to be stopped until one of them lay unmoving against the hard, cold earth.

Shell rolled away from the kick and then came to his feet, his back to the fire. Campbell rushed at him but Shell sidestepped, stabbing a left hand into Campbell's face three times in rapid succession, bringing blood from Hector's nostrils.

"I'll tear you apart! I'll rip your goddamned head off!" Hector roared. Saying it wasn't going to do it, however.

Campbell came in again, enraged, both fists held high beside his ears. Blood from the gunshot smeared one side of his face and there was beginning to be some puffiness around the eyes from Shell's jabbing left hand. He helped it along, sticking the straight left into Campbell's face again. Four times, five, six. A little *woof* of pain escaped Campbell's lips with each blow.

Shell was circling away, not wanting his back to the fire, to Sam Campbell and Jack Claypool. He felt the boot behind his ankle, but he never saw who it was that tripped him, and it was too late to recover. Shell went down on his back as Hector Campbell, his eyes lighting with savage joy, hurled himself at Morgan.

Shell managed to get a bent leg up and Campbell was kicked up and over, Shell gripping the big man's shirt at the collar, shoving out with his boot.

Campbell landed on his back in the campfire. Golden sparks shot into the air, cinders flew everywhere. Campbell screamed with pain and rolled from the fire, spreading sparks across the earth. His shirt was on fire briefly, but he rolled it out as Morgan got to his feet, hovering over him, waiting.

"Bastard, bastard, bastard," Campbell breathed. Hector was displaying a very limited imagination tonight.

"Get up, Hector," Shell invited. "Let's finish it. Or are you done?"

"Done, hell," Campbell shrieked like a kid whose voice is just changing, and he hurled himself at Shell's legs, meaning to take him down to the ground, to use his superior weight to maul, to overwhelm the taller, leaner Morgan.

It didn't work out real well.

Campbell lunged and Shelter brought his knee up. There was a sickening crack as Hector's nose met Morgan's kneecap and something gave. The big man rolled away, legs kicking with pain, hands clasped to his nose.

"Give it up, Hector," Shell said. "It's not worth it, friend."

It was worth it to Hector. He got up again, staggering forward, his face a mask of blood now as it streamed from the broken nose. His eyes were puffed around dark, narrow slits, his cheekbone was split in two places, cut to the bone by the razor-like blows of Shelter Morgan.

"You got to die, Morgan, you got to go down," Hector said, and he dragged himself forward.

Morgan moved back and away, jabbing still, keeping the big man off him. Hector Campbell wasn't bright and he wasn't real good with his fists, but he was determined. He was real determined—Shell had heard of men who didn't have the sense to know when to quit, but he had seldom run into one quite this obstinate.

Shell had the man beat, and he knew it. Still he didn't discount Campbell's cunning, his strength. He was wary still and it was fortunate that he was.

The knife had appeared from nowhere, filling Campbell's hand. Ten inches of narrow, razor-edged blade protruded from a stag horn handle and Hector swept the weapon slowly back and forth before him.

Shell's own bowie hung from a sheath at the back of his belt and he reached for it now, but he never got it out. Arms clamped around him, an iron hard grip that had to belong to Sam Campbell. Shell could hear the big man breathing—a chuckling little sound—he could smell the whiskey and coffee breath of Sam Campbell, and in front of him Hector Campbell, eyes gleaming, face bloody and bruised, shirt torn, came in, the knife glinting in the firelight.

"I want you men to stop this! Now!"

Thornhill had to have been joking, Shell thought. There was only one way the marshal could have stopped them and that was to shoot them dead.

Sam Campbell's grip was tightening around Shell's chest, cutting the air off, constricting the flow of blood. Shell's head began to swim. He had to move, and move he did.

He jammed his skull back into Campbell's face, hearing a nose crack. Simultaneously he kicked back savagely with his bootheel, catching the shin just below the knee and Sam Campbell gave up the bear hug to spin away, gripping his knee and nose at once.

Hector Campbell, afraid he'd miss his chance, hurried his attempt.

He slashed out wildly with the knife in his hand, missing by bare inches. Shell's shirt was sliced open from side to side. A thin trickle of blood appeared across his hard-muscled belly, but Hector had blown his chance and he knew it.

The knife hand slashed past Shell from left to right and as it got to its farthest point Shell grabbed for and found Campbell's wrist with both hands. He twisted hard and came up behind Campbell, ducking under his arm. Then the hand was folded back on itself, back until the fingers slowly opened and the knife dropped free.

Shell was suddenly weary of it, very weary. He kicked Hector Campbell behind the knee with all the force he could muster and the big man dropped to the ground in horrible pain. When he tried to rise Shell cut loose with the blow he had been holding back, saving for the right opening.

It was a big curving hook, a beautiful thing that caught Hector Campbell on the jaw hinge and sent a jolting message to his brain: Close up shop.

Hector blinked and his legs sagged at the knees. Then he fell forward, Shell stepping aside to let him crash to the ground on his battered face and lay there twitching spasmodically.

Shell spun drawing his gun. Sam Campbell was behind him, blood leaking from his nose. Sam shook his head almost sorrowfully and turned away. He had had enough. To one side Jack Claypool stood, arms folded, black eyes amused. No, Claypool wasn't one for aimless brawling, he was a professional all the way, and Shelter realized, the most dangerous one of them all.

Shell holstered his gun and staggered back toward the fire. He found his hat and put it on. Then he fished the coffee pot out of the coals and poured himself a cup. He sat there on his haunches, slowly drinking it in the utter silence, all eyes watching him.

When he was through he rose, glanced once at Hector

79

Campbell who had made it to a sitting position and was now propped up watching the blood leak from his nose to the earth beneath him.

Without a word Morgan turned and walked out of the ring of firelight toward the spot where he had left his bedroll. He was tired, stiff and battered—more than he would have wanted anyone to know.

He picked up his bedroll and moved to a new spot not far from his hobbled horses, above them. Then he stood for a long while in the darkness, looking back toward the fire, waiting.

For he knew they would come again. You don't whip a Campbell and expect him to shake hands and apologize. Their minds don't work that way.

Hector would be back. Again and again. Not so incautiously next time, perhaps. Maybe from ambush—a Winchester was as good a way as any. It wasn't over. It wouldn't be until one of them was buried in whatever kind of shallow grave could be scraped in the harsh soil of the desert.

Shelter turned in, his Colt in hand, and he lay watching the stars for a long while, thinking of Joe Bass, not making much sense out of that, not quite figuring this kid who had taken his outlaw father's name, kidnapped his own sister.

Then for a time Shelter thought of Merri Richardson—that was a whole lot easier thinking and he fell to sleep with her still on his mind.

It was already warm, dry when Shell rolled out at dawn. There was some dew down in the canyon, sparkling in the morning light, but that wouldn't last long.

Shell slid down into the gulley, saddled up the roan and led his horses back up to the main camp. He was stiff, his hands swollen and sore. A pair of ribs down low on the right side hurt horribly. He couldn't recall having been hit there.

He walked to the fire and squatted down, reaching for the coffee pot. You could almost hear the silence grow taut as he did so. Inwardly Shelter smiled.

The Campbell's weren't around. Just Claypool, sardonic and dark, and the Indian.

"They rode out early," Dave Becker said. The kid was excited. Life is a great adventure. Hooray. "Both of 'em with big swollen-up noses. Hector's is broken, though I don't think Sam's is. God, Morgan, if you knew the times people backed down to those two in Jacumba . . . well, even myself," the kid shrugged.

"Where's the marshal?"

"He went out early too, circling the camp to look for sign. Doubt he'll cut any. Damn, that was a fight!"

"Uh-huh." Shell sipped at his coffee. His head ached dully behind the eyes.

"Some of the boys were saying it was luck that you cut the lobe of Hector's ear with that .44, they say no one could've done it in that light, without hardly aimin' like you did."

"Do they?" Shell took another drink of coffee. He liked the kid, he honestly did, but Dave was talking himself right out of a relationship. Morgan tried to recall how it was when he was young and excitable, when the guns and the excitement were fun and not pure cold business, and he only half-succeeded.

There had once been a barefoot boy who had signed up to go to war, inflamed with the thrill of it, wanting a fancy new uniform, one of those rifle-muskets they were handing out so new they smelled of tool oil and packing grease.

81

He could recall that kid—his name had been Shelter Morgan too—but it had been so long ago, so far away, that he was only one of the many ghosts Morgan carried with him, would carry with him until some fool like Hector Campbell or some hardnosed professional like Jack Claypool finally got the plug in him.

"So was it?" Dave Becker asked eagerly. "I had money on it, you see."

"Was what, kid?"

"Was it luck that you got Hector Campbell's earlobe?"

"Yeah. Pure luck," Shell said. "I was aiming for his big toe."

The kid was almost but not quite sure he was kidding. The discussion got no further. Someone raised a shout and heads turned toward the east. The marshal was coming in and he was coming in at a good clip.

Shell stood squinting into the sun. No, there was no pursuit, but the marshal was definitely excited. When he reined up in front of them, white alkali dust sifting through the air, they found out why.

"I cut his sign out a mile and a half, toward the Big Tanks." Thornhill said, dabbing at his dusty face.

Someone hoorahed and a cooler head asked, "You sure, Jeb?"

"Of course I'm sure. I've seen Joe Bass' sign before. That blue roan he rides has a turned out hind foot and a chip in the front shoe. At least it did two days ago.

"Let's get the son of a bitch," someone said over-eagerly. Shell, glancing around at the voice saw that the two Campbell brothers had drifted back into camp. Both had badly swollen noses. Hector's face was chopped up good. "Good," Shell thought maliciously. It was partial repayment for the way he felt inside this morning.

"Hold on a minute," the marshal said, mastering his own eagerness. "I found that sign in an old wadi. Printed in mud and baked in there. It's got to be at least a day old, maybe two. We're heading the right way, men, but we're not going to get on our horses and ride him down this morning. This is going to take a while. I told you that when we started out. Now then—let's finish up our breakfast and get on that bastard's trail."

They finished up their breakfast and got on Joe Bass' trail. Shell rode with Dave Becker for a time and then drifted off to the south to ride to the right and behind the body of the posse. He wanted no further discussions with the Campbells.

The country was dry salt playa. The horses' hoofs broke through the thin, ancient layer of salt as they moved. No dust rose, no breeze stirred. Ahead the mountains, deep brown, corrugated, loomed. They never seemed to draw any nearer.

There was just nothing growing in that area with the exception of a barrel cactus here and there. A horse stepped onto the long spines of one and was gimped up. From then on everyone rode wary.

They camped at noon, if you could call it a camp. They changed saddles, looked at each other's sun-baked, salt-rimmed faces and sat panting in the shade of their mounts sipping canteen water.

Shelter watched their faces, wondering how long they would put up with deprivation. They weren't tough, these play-soldiers from Jacumba. None of them were but for the Campbells and their friends. Shell had no respect at all for the mentality of Hector Campbell, but it was difficult not to give him high marks for tenacity. Jack Claypool looked as if he were out for a Sunday ride. Cool, lean, his dark face calm. His sights were set on five thousand dollars.

Or could there have been something else Claypool wanted out of this?

During the ride Shell had pondered Claypool and the rest of the possible opposition. He thought he remembered the man now—remembered him from Texas where there had been a flare-up between two rival ranches. A man named Claypool had been killed during that range war. Shelter knew that. He had seen him go down before his own sights.

The afternoon was hot and nearly painful, the sun hammering down, the air so arid that it was uncomfortable to breathe. The desert flats shimmered and dazzled the eye, the horses plodded on, heads down.

They found the village at sundown.

Nestled in the rattlesnake-infested foothills it couldn't have been more than half inhabited. There were a dozen sun-baked buildings on the cactus stippled slopes. Most of them seemed to be on the verge of tumbling down.

"Chanticleer," Dave Becker said as the posse sat the sundown ridge, letting the horses blow. There was a whisper of wind moving over the desert now. Out on the flats a little fine dust began to move, here in the foothills which were an unexpected knob thrust up out of the white flats, there was enough breeze to term it that. Shell could feel the sweat trickling down from his armpits, feel the wind touch his damp throat.

"What's that?" Shell asked.

"Chanticleer?" Dave Becker laughed. He hadn't learned all of his grown-up manners yet. "Just a filthy Indian town. The railroad had an idea of building a spur out this way once. There was a borax mine, you see.

84

Owned by Western Consolidated. Just about the time the railroad got the work camp built the borax ran out."

"That's what Chanticleer is? A railroad work camp?"

"It was going to be. No laborers ever got here. After the railroad pulled off the Indians moved in—they're what you call Kikima Indians. Mostly they're farther south down on the Gulf."

"Hell of a place to live in."

"Nothing here. Nothing at all. Just the well, and that's what keeps the Indians here. The railroad sunk a good well, I'll give 'em that. Two hundred feet and perforated. So the Indians stay on. Why waste the water? You know how far it is between drinks out there . . ."

"Think he's in there, Marshal?" someone asked. There was a burr to the voice, an edge of anger, that kind of anger which comes from being exhausted, fed up.

"I don't know. If he is, we'll find him. Chanticleer isn't that much of a place."

"If he needed water . . ." someone began, letting his thoughts and voice fall silent.

"It's getting us nowhere talking," Sam Campbell said. "Let's ride on in and have our look."

The posse started forward then, a long line of dark horses, dark men moving slowly across the dusk-purpled hills. And God help the town of Chanticleer.

8.

Dave Becker had called it a town; Shelter wasn't willing to go that far. A half dozen toppling or toppled wooden buildings lined a cleared patch of ground which only imagination could make into a road. There was a huge boulder thrusting its head up through the center of this clearing, craggy, gray, indomitable.

Farther on was an adobe building with two blank windows staring out at the abandoned camp town. There was a sign in English and Spanish—"Saloon Cantina"— hanging from the log eaves.

The shadows were lying deep across the hills now and in the town of Chanticleer only the saloon was lighted. There might not have been anyone at all living in the other tumble-down buildings. Maybe there wasn't. But Shelter thought he saw dark, shadowy figures scuttling away into the deeper blackness as the posse trailed up the street, the clopping of their horses' hoofs loud against the packed and dry earth.

"How're we going to handle this, Marshal?"

The voice carried clearly through the darkness. It belonged to big Sam Campbell.

"I don't get you."

"He's here in this town."

"We don't know that, Sam." There was some irritation in the marshal's voice now.

"Where else is he going to be close to water out here?"

"We don't know where he is."

But Shelter had the idea the marshal did know. At least he knew where to leave the ransom money—something he couldn't admit without telling everyone that Yeats was carrying five thousand.

In his own mind Shelter had already dismissed Chanticleer as the place chosen by Joe Bass for a hideout or rendezvous. Where, then? It was a good question, for there wasn't a tablespoon of clear water for fifty miles in any direction that anyone seemed to know of; but then the old Indian had said that Joe Bass knew the desert like few but an Indian did. In the hills there could be springs, or *tinajas*—sheltered stone tanks, catch basins where sweet water stood most of the year. There could be—but no one in this party knew where there was any water unless someone was holding out.

If someone was Shelter didn't believe that Sam Campbell was in on the secret. The big redhead genuinely believed that Joe Bass was hiding in Chanticleer, or that he had at the least been through.

"Someone knows," Sam was muttering. "And someone will talk too."

"You lay off the locals," Thornhill said, but there

wasn't a lot of force in his command. Maybe because he realized that he and the townspeople from Jacumba didn't stack up real good against Campbell and his hard men. Maybe.

There was a brooding, weary silence among them now as the party reached the saloon and swung down. The horses shuddered and blew. Men slapped the dust from their clothing and stood looking at each other in the darkness, wishing they weren't there perhaps. Maybe a few of them were afraid—they should have been. By then they should have been.

They tramped up onto the swaying porch and went inside. Twenty trail-dusty men, and the heads of the locals, Indians all except for the bartender, stayed turned down to the tables. They knew, Shelter thought. The word had come to them long ago. They knew an army had descended.

The bartender looked up warily, saw the star of Jeb Thornhill's vest and broke into a smile of relief.

"Marshal Thornhill! A ways out of your area, aren't you?"

"I am. Wally Weese, isn't it?" The two men shook hands. "Ran into you down in Descanso once."

"You've got a good memory—but that was none of my doing!" Wally Weese held up a hand. "I swear it."

"All right. Forget it, I have. We're thirsty, Wally. What've you got?"

"Cerveza—Mexican cerveza just up from Mexicali, and good rye whiskey." Weese looked around at the crowd of Americans, his sun-burned round face holding that professional grin.

Sam Campbell wasn't shy. "Give me a gallon of that beer, barkeep, and a bottle on the side. I'm dry clear through, dry and weary."

The bartender didn't know Sam Campbell and he wasn't long on discretion. "Sure, friend. What happened to your nose? Walk into a door, did you?"

"Yeah," Sam Campbell said in a low, menacing drawl. "I walked into a door. And if you don't get your butt in gear and bring me my order you're going to walk into the floor, my friend."

"Sure." Weese held up apologetic hands. "Sorry, friend, no need to get excited. I'll serve you right up. The rest of you, call it out! Tell me what you want and I'll serve it up. I got all you want, plenty of it!"

Sam Campbell had turned slowly and now with one elbow on the bar he let his eyes rake Shelter Morgan for a minute. The big man hadn't forgotten. Not for a second.

Shelter waited for the mob to go first then he got himself a beer, walking with it to a corner table where the marshal sat with Yeats and another townie named Caffiter. They didn't seem real thrilled to have Shelter join them. It didn't matter, they were getting him.

The marshal, Morgan noticed, was dipping into a bottle of rye whiskey. By the flush on his face, the level of liquid in the bottle, he seemed to be dipping in awfully fast. You never knew—Shell hadn't pegged the lawman for a drinker.

"You men don't mind, do you?" Shell asked, reversing a chair to sit at the table, his arms folded on the chair back. Across the room the Campbells were having a high old time. The Indian that travelled with them was putting the liquor away almost as fast as the marshal. The bald-headed man was showing him a knife trick, the heavy blade thunking into the table top.

Around the perimeter of the room the locals began to

finish their drinks and slowly filter out of the saloon. They could smell trouble brewing. So could Shell.

"You ought to have steered clear of the cantina," Shell told the marshal.

He took it personally. "Can't a man have a damn drink, Morgan?"

"Sure. Those that can handle it."

"Are you saying I can't?" Thornhill stiffened. His red face grew redder.

"I wasn't talking about you, Thornhill. It never entered my mind. I'm talking about the Campbells and those with them. They're primed for trouble, and the last thing they needed was liquor."

"I've got my eye on them," the marshal growled. He had his eye on the whiskey, was where he had it, but Shell kept his mouth shut, shrugging.

"When you saw Joe Bass' tracks this morning," Shell asked, "was he riding alone?"

"That's right. Alone."

"Funny." Shelter sipped at his beer. Someone shouted across the room and they glanced that way. The knife game had gotten a little out of control. Someone was nicked, the Indian, it seemed.

"What's so funny about it?"

"Just that we know Bass didn't leave Jacumba alone. He had three or four men with him, Manta said. Plus the girl."

"So? It don't mean a thing. His horse just happened to be the one that stepped in the mud."

"Is that the way it was?"

"You men better take it easy now!" Wally Weese called out from behind the bar. He was trying to make his voice jocular, but it wasn't working well. Those boys were getting themselves fired up. It was the marshal's job to put a clamp on it, but he didn't seem much interested.

"They're getting a head of steam up, aren't they?" Yeats said quietly.

"Now you're takin' Morgan's side?" the marshal exploded. The violence of the retort caused the banker to jerk upright, frowning in confusion.

"Why, no, Jeb. I just . . ."

"You don't think I'm doing my job either, is that it?"

"Nothing of the kind," Yeats said smoothly. "I'd just hate to see things get out of hand."

"They're not getting out of hand. The men are unwinding a little." Someone unwound with a Colt .44 as the marshal spoke. The bullet splintered the wall behind the bar and Sam Campbell barked with laughter.

"This is getting too rough for me. Goodnight," Caffiter said. The marshal looked disdainfully at the townsman and threw back another shot of rye whiskey.

"I'm going with you," Yeats said. He looked from the marshal to the Campbells and back with some apprehension.

"Me too," Morgan said. He finished his beer and rose. "Why don't you come along and get some rest, Thornhill?"

"I'm not drunk," he said defensively.

"I didn't say you were. It's been a long trail and we've got some hard travelling ahead of us. Let's get some sleep," Shelter said mildly.

"You go to hell." The marshal's voice was distant, flat, slurred. Shelter turned to the others and shrugged.

"The marshal doesn't want to come, gentlemen."

"Come on, Yeats," Caffiter said. He was obviously nervous now. The party across the room was getting out of hand. The two Campbells were shouting and whistling while their bald-headed companion danced a heavy jig. The Indian was glassy-eyed, sitting there digging at the table with a long knife. Only Jack Claypool was silent, sober. The tall man sat there toying with his mustache, dark eyes gleaming as he watched Morgan and the two townies walk past and go out into the cool of the desert night.

"Fools," Yeats said with a savagery which surprised Morgan. The banker didn't look the type to lose his temper easily.

"It'll blow over," Caffiter said hopefully.

"When? The marshal's not going to be much good tomorrow, is he? And if we don't get this . . ."

Shelter finished it for him. "If we don't get this ransom money to Joe Bass when and where he demanded it, we're placing Dorothy Patch in real danger."

"Who says I've got ransom money with me?" Yeats said nervously.

"Come on." Shell glanced at the saloon, tilted his head and led Yeats and Caffiter off up the street a way. The stars overhead were brilliant. The rest of the town was utterly black and still. "Everyone knows it—ask your friend Caffiter here. Who else is carrying saddlebags around with him?

"That doesn't prove . . ."

"We know," Caffiter said as if embarrassed. "Me and the boys figured it out. Why would Mr. Scrivener let you out of the bank? Why would you ride along with a posse? Why hadn't anyone heard of Joe Bass sending a ransom note? No, Yeats, the man's right, everyone's figured it out."

"Say you're right," the banker said. "So what then?"

His voice was a little tight as he realized he was standing in the darkness with two men who knew he had five thousand in cash slung over his arm. His hand was slowly moving to settle near his waist gun. Shelter saw it and smiled thinly.

"Take it easy, Yeats. I don't want the money and I don't think Caffiter here does either. But there's some men in that saloon who do. My advice, if you'll let me give you some, is to hide yourself and that money out overnight, until this whiskey storm blows over and the marshal's back in shape to take charge.

"Hide out?" Yeats laughed. "What do you mean? There's a dozen of us and only five in the Campbell gang. You can't honestly think they'd try for the money."

"Why not? If they get you while you're sleeping you wouldn't have a chance. Hit quick and sprint for the border. How far is it? Twenty, twenty-five miles? There's no way any help could reach here from Jacumba. No way anyone would ever hear about it."

"You spin a wild yarn," Yeats said.

"Yes—and if I were you, I'd listen to it. I'm not trying to scare anyone, I'm just pointing out what could happen. Why the hell else do you think the Campbells are along on this posse? Think that over twice."

The saloon door opened up the street. A patch of light flooded the street for a moment, the sound of shouting and loud laughter rolled out of the open door before it was banged shut again. Two townsmen, disgusted apparently, started walking their way.

They stopped abruptly as they saw the three men in the dark.

"Who is that?" A coat flap was lifted, a hand reached for a gun.

"Yeats. I've got Morgan and Caffiter here with me."

"Yeats. All right." The newcomer was trying to disguise his nervousness and not doing it well. They came nearer. "Those fools are talking of tearing the town open. Sam Campbell is convinced that Joe Bass is hiding here, that he has to be. There's no water for miles outside of Chanticleer, he says."

"Can the marshal keep the lid on?"

"The marshal, my friend, doesn't seem to know where he is right now."

"Then it's up to us," Yeats said.

"Up to us?"

"Yes. To protect the town from the Campbell gang."

"The hell it is. I didn't join up with this posse to protect a bunch of indigent Kikima Indians from a gang of drunken toughs. I'm out here to find Joe Bass, that's it."

"But Chanticleer . . ."

"Screw Chanticleer! What's the difference if it burns to the ground? The wind'll blow it flat within a year. The well will dry up, the Indians will drift back south where they came from. Who cares if Sam Campbell does it this year or nature does it next year?"

"Who cares about the Indians?" Yeats asked with a tenacity Shelter admired.

"Squatters. Desert rats. They'll clear out before anything can happen. They know how to take care of themselves. I damn sure won't die for them. And that," he concluded, "is that."

The two men walked off, leaving Yeats, Caffiter and Morgan alone again.

"That's going to be the general opinion," Caffiter offered. "Who's going to stand up in front of Campbell and his toughs and tell them what they can do and can't do anyway?" He sounded disconsolate, slightly ashamed.

"He's right, Morgan. Besides, maybe nothing will happen. Hell," Yeats said with a dry laugh, "nothing's going to happen. It's the liquor talking, that's all."

"Sure." Morgan was staring back at the saloon.

"It's only whiskey talk," Caffiter agreed. "The worst thing we could do would be to stand around and watch them as if we were policing them. They'd take it as a challenge, wouldn't they?"

Morgan nodded in the darkness. They were convincing themselves that there wasn't anything in Chanticleer worth fighting for, dying for, and that was always an easy argument to win.

"Let's turn in, Morgan."

"You men go ahead. I'll linger for a time."

"If you . . . I mean, if you want someone to stay with you," Yeats said.

"No. You go on. Just recall what I told you. When they come out of that saloon they're going to be walking tall, walking mean. If they take a notion to have that gold, they'll have it. You men find a quiet camp and keep the fires out."

"If you really . . ."

"That's what I really think. That's the way it's really going to be, damnit!" Shelter said, letting his anger show through for the first time. At times he wondered how they had ever gotten this country from the Indians. Their fathers must have been a different breed. Men willing to fight when the time came, to die if need be.

"You go on along," Shell repeated more quietly and the two townsmen moved off without any more protests.

Shelter watched them go, then slowly he crossed the street and walked to where the big boulder jutted up in the center of town. There he crouched down, listening to the darkness, watching the saloon where drunken echoes sounded.

Hours passed and the noise got louder, rougher. The last few townsmen gave it up and left, staggering slightly toward their horses. That left only the marshal and the Campbell gang inside the saloon.

Another hour with the stars swinging slowly past, the creaking, settling sounds of old buildings, the occasional burst of noise from the saloon.

Shelter was alone in the darkness, or seemed to be, but from time to time something moved in the shadows. Something he could sense but not see, undefined, flitting, animal-like.

But it wasn't an animal—of that he was sure, although he couldn't have said why.

The saloon door banged open and the bald-headed man stormed out, Sam Campbell at his shoulder, Hector Campbell behind him, his voice booming out.

"Find him and kill him! He's here and they're hiding him. Let's dig him out!"

They moved off of the saloon steps, the three of them, and still Morgan did not move. He remained crouching beside the giant boulder, looking for the dangerous one, the deadly one. Jack Claypool who was sober and more of a threat than these other three put together. But Claypool didn't come.

It had been silent in the darkness, now suddenly that silence was shattered. Shelter heard the sounds of boards being ripped from their moorings, of doors being kicked in, locks shot from them. The sounds of a town preparing to die.

9.

As the four men went past Shelter they split up, the Campbell brothers moving to his right, the Indian and the fourth thug to his left. Then they moved down the street, determined to find Joe Bass if he was concealed in that town.

Shelter looked toward the saloon again. Still there was no sign of Jack Claypool, and none of the marshal. But the way Thornhill had been putting the booze down the battle of Gettysburg wouldn't wake him.

The townies had made their position clear—it wasn't their business. Maybe it wasn't Shell's either, but he wasn't going to let the Kikimas' town be torn down for no good reason.

What he was going to do wasn't clear. When the scream sounded in the night his decision was made for him. That was a woman screaming, and she was in mortal terror.

Shell was to his feet and sprinting in the direction of the scream in seconds. He ordered things in his mind as he ran, Colt in hand.

Behind him were the Campbell brothers. That meant the Indian and the bald-headed thug were involved in this, singly or together. Two of them. One would be busy with the woman.

But where the hell was she?

Shell looked around him, seeing nothing. He hit the boardwalk in front of the old work barracks and plunged inside the darkened building, seeing the door torn off at the hinges.

He could see nothing inside, nothing at all. Shell crouched, panting in the darkness, eyes scouring the interior, finding nothing. He rose and started across the room, planks squeaking underfoot.

Moving through an interior doorway he heard another noise—a soft sobbing, muffled, near at hand.

He saw the man step out of the shadows and raise a weapon. Shelter's Colt bucked in his hand and the man screamed, throwing up his hands, stumbling back against the wall behind him.

By the muzzle flash Shelter had seen him—the bald-headed man with his pants down smothering the young Indian woman with his bulky body. Now he lurched to his feet, trying to hobble away with his pants around his ankles.

Shelter let him get to his rifle which was tilted against the wall beneath a window, then he shot him. Shot him twice through his fat body and watched him fall, feeling not a drop of pity for the bastard.

Shelter crossed the room, holstering his gun. The Indian girl cowered in the corner, holding a hand up before her face.

"Come on," Morgan said. When she hesitated, he yanked her roughly to her feet. Those gunshots would bring the Campbells on the run.

In the corner the Indian was thrashing and moaning still. Shelter thought he had taken lead in the arm high up, but he wasn't sure and he wasn't going to take the time to find out now.

They had reached the window and the girl hesitated, dragging her feet. Shelter picked her up and tossed her out bodily, following himself seconds later. He could hear the sound of boots rushing across the wooden floor of the barracks, and holding the stunned girl to the ground he lifted his Colt up over the sill of the window, firing three times at random. The Campbells reversed directions rapidly, one of them—Hector?—growling a curse.

"Come on."

Shell jerked the girl to her feet and, running at a crouch, led her off into the cactus-dotted hills behind Chanticleer. He glanced back only once but there was no pursuit. The Campbells had been warned off and it was doubtful they would want to pursue anyone with a gun through the darkness.

Shell crested a little ridge. His hand was cramped from gripping the woman's wrist so tightly. She twisted and clawed at his hand as they moved, struggling to be free, apparently wanting to run back to the town.

"Damn you!" she hissed and Shelter, turning toward her, grinned.

"English, bless my soul."

"Damn you!" Then again, maybe she didn't know much English, only a few choice words.

"Listen, woman, I don't want to hurt you, understand?" Shell crouched down and he forced the girl to crouch too, looking at her with intent eyes. "That man was no friend of mine. I'm not going to hurt you, but you've got to promise me you're not going back down to that town again. Tell me that, and I'll let you go. Do you understand me?"

"She doesn't, but I do," the soft voice from behind Shelter Morgan said. Shell felt the sort hairs curl up a little, the cold fingers run down his spine. The man was very, very good to come up on Morgan like that, unseen, unheard. Slowly he turned.

He looked to be between eighty and a hundred years old, wrinkled, bent, dried up as old leather, his hands big and gnarled wrapped around the old musket-rifle he carried. Shelter let go of the girl and she rushed to the old man, crying, burying her face against his shoulder, speaking in a tongue Shell didn't understand.

"She thought I was down there," the old man said. "She went back to look for me. She is a good girl, Kolka, and she would not leave her grandfather in time of trouble."

"Kolka is her name?"

"Yes."

"Mine is Shelter Morgan."

The girl turned, lowered a finger at Shelter and said again, "Damn you!" her voice a sibilant whisper.

"No." The old man took the girl's chin and turned it toward him. Rapidly he explained something in the Kikima tongue and the girl glanced toward Shelter, nodding. "I have told her that you are a good man. I have told her that you did not wish to hurt her," the old Indian said. "It is fortunate for you that this is so. My people are not warlike, stranger, but I know many ways of making pain."

"I believe you. I hope you also know how to make friends."

"A friend of mine is a friend for my life," the old man said. "But now we must go. There are others in the town who are not friendly."

"Where will you go?"

"Into the hills, onto the desert." The old man shrugged. "The desert winds will blow away those who have come tonight and when they are gone we will return."

Shelter was only half-listening. He was looking at the girl, Kolka. By starlight she was a rarely beautiful thing, proud and sleek. She wore a white blouse which revealed fine firm breasts, and a dark skirt. Her hair was gathered together at the base of her skull, not braided. She had a broad mouth but a narrow nose for an Indian. There was some Spanish blood not far back in her.

"God damn!" Kolka said suddenly and she pointed excitedly. Shelter turned to face the town, seeing the fire leap into the night sky. The old work barracks were tinder-dry; the flames devoured them voraciously. Sparks gouted skyward, the crackling of the fire was audible even on the distant ridge where Shelter stood with the two Kikima Indians.

"God damn," Kolka repeated. Her face was brightened by the fire. Wide dark eyes looked down onto the flats with unhappy intentness.

"It does not matter," the old man said. "So long as the water is good. If the water remains then it is a good place for us. We will build new shelters."

Morgan was aware of the others now, sifting out of the

101

hills, drifting like shadows to gather around the old man. There were upwards of thirty Kikima Indians in the tribe, half of them women, a few holding babies.

The fire had really taken hold now. The adobe saloon of Wally Weese was apparently safe, being made of clay bricks and separated from the rest of the town. The rest of it was doomed. Shelter wondered what the Kikimas had left behind down there, what prized possessions.

"May I ask you something?" Shell said.

"Yes." The old man stood silently watching the flames.

"The reason your town was destroyed was because they thought you had sheltered an outlaw, a man they are looking for. Do you understand me?"

"Hanapa understands," the old man replied.

"Yes. I want to find this man too, Hanapa. I want to capture him because he has stolen a woman and he threatens to kill her. Have you seen a man riding through here?"

"No man."

"Please. It's important. A young man with a woman hostage. Perhaps there were four or five men in a group, all from the west."

"What is it you want with this man?" Hanapa asked.

"I told you what I wanted." Shell read the uncertainty in the old Indian's eyes. "Are we not friends, Hanapa?" he asked quietly.

"Yes," the old man's eyes turned down. "We are friends. I saw these men. Four men. One woman."

"She was all right?"

"Yes. They came not yesterday, but one day before, in the morning. They watered their horses and rode on."

"Which direction?" Shell asked, trying to keep his

voice calm.

"That way." Hanapa inclined his head. "Into the hills, into the hills. Look for them there. That is all I know."

And that was all Shelter wanted to know. Joe Bass wasn't far off. He was in the nearby hills with the girl, and so far Dorothy Patch was alive.

Shelter thanked the Kikimas and watched them filter off into the night, going God knows where. She hesitated. She hesitated and then walked up to him, not knowing what to say. Her eyes were firebright, huge. She wanted to speak but didn't know how. Her hand stretched out, rested for a moment on Shelter's chest and then was withdrawn as she looked up at him.

"Goodbye," Shell said.

"Goodbye." She said it wrong, all wrong, consonants slurred, vowels swallowed, but it was as nice a sounding word as anyone had ever voiced.

She looked at him a moment longer and then turned away, walking to where her grandfather stood waiting. Together they walked into the night and were swallowed up by it and after a minute there was no sound in the night but the angry crackling of flames and even that was dying away as the town of Chanticleer died unmourned out on the empty desert.

Shell was up at dawn. The scent of dead ash was heavy on the morning breeze. He walked to the campfire to find Dave Becker, Caffiter, Yeats and a battered appearing Marshal Jeb Thornhill hunkered over the little bit of warmth it offered against the cool of the desert morning.

"Morning," Shelter said, pouring himself a cup of coffee.

"Good morning," Dave Becker said. No one else felt much like talking apparently. The marshal sure didn't.

103

His face was gray, lifeless, his eyes pouched, bleary. His hand shook as he lifted the coffee cup to his lips.

If a man looked close enough he could see something else worrying the marshal, something way down deep, but Shelter couldn't figure out what it was. Not then.

"I was hoping you were all right," young Dave Becker told Shell. He had his hat off and his curly blond hair was flying out in all directions.

"All right? Why?" Shell asked blandly.

"Why, man, last night was the damnedest thing I ever seen! Whole town burned down before my eyes. You were gone. There's talk," the kid said confidentially, "that the Campbells fired the town."

"The Campbells?" Shell was suitably impressed.

"That's right, so I was wonderin' where in hell you were and what had happened."

"Well, I appreciate that, Dave. It's kind of nice to have someone worry about you."

The kid shrugged, a little embarrassed. "Baldy Schumann was killed."

"Schumann? Oh, that bald-headed man who tagged along with Campbell."

"That's right. Schumann was killed and the Apache was wounded in the shoulder."

"Is that right? What happened?"

"A couple of those Kikimas had guns," Dave said, lowering his voice, leaning forward. "Baldy and the Apache were tearing up their home and the Kikimas didn't take to it."

"Shut up," Marshal Thornhill snarled.

Becker's head jerked around with surprise. He gawked at the marshal. "Why, what's the matter, Marshal?"

"Nothin'. Just quit talking, that's all. My head hurts."

104

"You paid a lot for that headache, Marshal," Shell cracked, "you enjoy it all you can."

"Shut up."

"Sure," Morgan shrugged, winking at Dave Becker.

"You shouldn't have come on this party, Morgan. You're in the wrong place, you know that." The marshal was staring at the fire, not at Morgan.

"Am I?"

"You know damned well you are. This isn't your affair. Why don't you pull off now? Take the kid with you."

"What's he talking about?" Dave Becker asked.

"Nothing. It's the whiskey talking still, isn't it, Marshal?" Shell answered.

"Sure." Thornhill looked at Becker and then let his eyes shuttle away. "Only the whiskey talking."

The sun was an orange ball hanging above the jagged edge of the mountain range when the party rode out again. The coolness of the desert morning lasted only for an hour, then it turned hot, fiendishly hot and they slogged on, the horses dragging.

"Is there water in those hills or not?" Dave Becker asked. Morgan could only shrug. No one with them seemed to know. It didn't matter. You sat your saddle, the sun baking you and you rode on, on until you fell or darkness came.

The land began to uptilt. There was less sand now, more volcanic rock—like black glass it sliced at the hoofs of the horses and had to be detoured around. But the only detours were rock- and cactus-clogged canyons twisting and narrow, thick with rattlers. They buzzed on every side, joining the cicadas and the desert toads, the humming gnats in a maddening serenade.

"Look here." It was Caffiter who yelled out and in minutes they were gathered around him to stare at the prize.

A dark blue kerchief, faded and torn, rested on a sprig of sumac and they stood looking at it as if it were a fortune. The sweat ran off the marshal's body, soaking his shirt. He smelled raw and unhealthy.

"They came this way."

"You know who owned that?" Shell asked cautiously.

"What?" The marshal's eyes sharpened. His face was dead white with crimson spots on the cheeks. "No, I don't know who owned it, Morgan. But who else would be riding out this way?"

"I don't know. I just didn't want everyone getting too excited. When people get too excited, they start shooting."

"You're the only one getting excited," Sam Campbell drawled. The big man still sat his horse though the rest of them had leaped down. Now he stood casting a thick shadow across Shelter Morgan's face.

"Maybe," Shell shrugged.

"It had to come from the Joe Bass gang," the marshal insisted.

"Why? Because they're the only ones who could have come this way? You're telling me the scarf has to be theirs because only they would ride this way; that they had to have ridden this way because you've got a scarf. Marshal—your logic isn't real strong."

"Screw you and your logic, Morgan," Thornhill said. "I don't know what you're trying to prove and I doubt you do."

"Just trying to examine things logically, carefully, without accepting everything at face value—that's important, wouldn't you say, Marshal?"

The marshal felt disinclined to answer. They swung aboard again and started on up the long canyon which led to a low, nearly barren plateau. Here and there a broken twisted oak or gnarled sycamore clung to a tentative existence among the rocks, but mostly it was low-growing sumac, sage, some nopal cactus, the lower pads chewed off by jack rabbits.

It was already within an hour of sundown when they achieved the plateau and stopped for a breather. A dry wind whipped across the flat bench. There were acres of nopal cactus there, much manzanita to the north where the plateau ended and the chocolate colored foothills began their climb into the blue desert sky. To the south nothing much seemed to grow. Broken hills, black rock outcroppings, barrel cactus, some greasewood.

The wind was dry but it cooled Shell's heated body as it swept across horses and men. Most everyone had swung down but for some reason Sam Campbell was still on his horse and so Shelter stayed in the saddle as well. Campbell noticed this and smiled—if you could call twisting his mouth up on one side smiling.

Hector Campbell drank from his canteen, drank as if there were deep, cool lakes all around them, that they had nothing but water. It ran down his whiskered chin and stained his shirt darkly.

You're in the wrong place, Morgan, the marshal had said. In the wrong place. Shelter couldn't put a handle on that. He sat looking around at the broad plateau, at the mountains above them, at the thirsty weary men.

The Apache, as he called himself, sat on the ground near his pinto pony, his shirt ripped open, his shoulder bandaged, glaring at Morgan. He knew all right. Knew or

107

had a suspicion.

The wind whispered through the low brush, making dry, rattling sounds.

You're in the wrong place.

The party mounted up again and they rode on. Still eastward, always eastward, riding the skirt of the chocolate mountains as the sun at their backs paled and colored and the nightbirds began to take to wing.

They dipped into the brush-filled hollow, all weary, all bent, their eyes on their horses' ears, waiting for someone to call a camp stop. They were thirsty and hungry—even the canned beans would taste almighty good. Even the ground would make a welcome bed. Their clothing was stiff with dried perspiration, filthy with days of dust. Their skin was chapped and gritty. Eyes red-rimmed, sore from peering into the desert sun hour after hour, day after day.

Shelter could see the Campbells in the lead, the marshal not far back. Then Cool Jack Claypool and the Apache. Then Caffiter and the rest of the townsmen. Directly in front of Morgan was Yeats, his horse tiring quickest because of the extra weight it carried—five thousand in gold. At Shell's right hand was Dave Becker, talking about his girlfriend back in Jacumba, something about her cute little pink ear.

He was still talking when the outlaws broke on them.

10.

It was a moment before things registered. The marshal had halted, seemed to say something to Sam Campbell, then they turned in unison at the head of the draw to look back down on those below, those caught in the brushy ravine.

Something rang a bell in Morgan's head, way back in a corner of the brain. Something he had seen before, something . . . . Georgia!

You don't belong here. Shell turned in the saddle and he saw them riding up the backtrail, black silhouettes against the orange dying sun. Half a dozen horsemen riding hard now, and in their hands steel glinted.

"Ambush!" Shelter shouted and the party was thrown into mad confusion.

The men in the canyon grabbed for their guns, but they were too slow about it. The first volley from behind took three men from the saddle. One of them was dragged away screaming by his horse as his foot slipped through the stirrup and wedged there.

Still they might have made a fight of it, but most of them didn't seem to realize that the firing was being aimed at them from both ends of the gorge.

Shell saw the Campbells levering shots through their guns as quick as they could work the action, saw the Apache fire into the face of Caffiter and blow him from the saddle.

"What the hell is it!" Dave Becker shouted hysterically and then he jerked upright as a bullet plowed through his chest and he toppled from the saddle to lie there, his blond, curly hair stained with blood.

Shell fired back with his Winchester, tagging a man behind them. He went behind his horse and then felt it shudder as it was hit. The little roan staggered and then went down, Shelter leaping free, grabbing frantically for the gray's lead line.

He swung up onto the bare back of the gray, still firing downslope, trying to carve a way out of the canyon.

Yeats still sat his horse although it was turning in a bewildered circle, throwing off the banker's aim. It didn't matter very much—Yeats wasn't much of a shot, and in another minute it didn't matter at all.

The bullet caught him in the mouth and angled up, lifting the back of Yeat's skull off, spraying Shelter with blood as the banker fell, his hands grabbing at the air reflexively.

All around the dead and dying moaned. The smell of burned gunpowder was rank in the air. A horse nickered, fell onto its side and tried to rise. It didn't make it and it lay pawing at the air in its death run as the guns fired from above and from below, as the canyon was swallowed up by sunset, by death's shadows.

Morgn grabbed the reins to Yeat's horse and swung away downslope. They weren't going to profit by this, damn them all! They weren't going to get that gold.

Behind Shelter a crackling volley sounded and he felt the angry pain in the small of his back. He'd been tagged and he knew it. How bad he didn't know, didn't want to know. Not just yet. He didn't have the time to think about it, to surrender to pain.

He was riding low across the gray's withers, leading Yeats' sorrel. Ahead the sun was only a softly glowing memory against the dark sky. There was nothing to be seen except the rough outlines of the giant landforms, the serrated ridges, the shoulder of the mountain to his right.

Then suddenly there was something else. The man popped up in front of Shell, rising Indian-like from the ground and Shelter saw the hot rose of his muzzle flash, felt the heat of the near shot.

But the man had been too anxious, to eager to claim his blood money perhaps, and Morgan thrust his Colt out, triggering it directly into the man's face as he rode past, as the outlaw's hands clutched at him trying to drag him from the saddle.

The outlaw was jerked back as if by wires, his face dissolving in a smear of blood and Shell was suddenly free, riding out of the canyon onto the long plateau while the guns spoke ceaselessly behind him.

They spoke angry words, chasing him into the darkness, but already he was nearly out of range and in a minute more he was lost to their eyes and the last shots were only bloody wishes.

111

Shelter didn't slow his pace. The big gray ran on blindly, moving toward the hills, the hills where there was cover, or the chance of it, Shelter's heels digging into the horse's ribs, constantly prodding, needing to make it far enough, fast enough, to be somewhere, anywhere where he would have a chance when he went down.

And that wasn't going to be long. The pain was swarming up his back, stabbing at his ribs with iron daggers, ripping at his organs with red-hot pincers.

He rode. The horse was in wild, fearful flight from something it didn't understand. Shell, clinging to it bareback, had knotted his hand into its mane. His legs were cramped and lifeless as he struggled to maintain his perch, as the gray leaped a rocky gulley, clambered up a long, brush covered slope and finally, wearily, simply halted.

If he had beat the gray it would have gone on, it would have run itself to death, but Shell wasn't going to do that. He wasn't going to lose that horse, damnit, because it was all he had out here.

He slowly slid from the gray to stand trembling beside it in the darkness, leaning against it for support.

Yeats' sorrel looked at him mournfully. It had had a good long run too, even without man-weight on its back. It had the gold and that was a load.

"Damn that gold," Shelter heard himself saying as he worked his way toward the sorrel. "Damn every gold-strike ever made, every mule-headed prospector and every bloody vein God planted in this earth."

They kept dying for it. He had practically relived the Conasauga ambush back there, relived the horror of war, of treachery. For gold they had died. For gold men had turned to murder.

It was enough to make him want to take that gold and scatter it across the broken hills, to bury it deep so that it wouldn't be the cause of more killing.

"Can't do it," Shell panted. He leaned his head against the sorrel's shoulder. "Just can't do that, Morgan. There's a girl's life riding on that gold. If Joe Bass doesn't get that gold then he's going to do some murder of his own."

Shell looked back down the hillslope, listening to the night sounds. He heard no pursuit, saw no one. It didn't mean much. He wasn't seeing too well. His head spun and his eyes weren't focusing. It was a dark night anyway. Moonless, airless, silent.

He must have lost them, but that would only be temporary. There was too much at stake. Not only the gold mattered here. There was a noose poised to settle around each man's neck if Shelter lived to tell his story.

If he lived . . . he lifted his shirt up out of his trousers and fingered the wound low on his back. Touching it brought on a wracking spasm of pain, and his knees nearly buckled.

It had gone right on through, he thought, without causing serious damage. His body didn't seem to realize that it hadn't suffered badly, however. Blood filled his pantleg, pain burst in little clusters behind his eyes.

Shell took his spare shirt from his saddlebags and tore it into strips. That wasn't as easy as it sounds. Moving hands and arms enough to accomplish that caused agonizing pain to stab through the lower back.

It wasn't any easier to wash the wound with canteen water and bind it, but finally Shelter had done that. They weren't going to award him any medical diploma for his work, but it was the best he could do.

When he was through he stood there shaking, his mind blurred, thoughts drifting.

"The mountains," he said out loud. He had to get into the mountains and find a place to hole up until he could get some strength back. He wasn't going to outrun anybody, but he could hold them off until . . . until what? There wasn't going to be any help coming, not out here. If help did come, why it was Morgan's word against the marshal's, and he knew which way that would go.

"And there's the girl." He looked upslope again, at the raw dark forms of the chocolate mountains. There was the girl.

Somewhere up there Dorothy Patch waited on this night, waited and hoped and maybe prayed a little. Someone would come, she thought. Someone who could take her home. But that someone was bleeding badly—and he didn't know where the meeting place was, where Yeats had been instructed to take the gold.

But Thornhill did, and he likely knew these mountains a hell of a lot better than Shelter.

"High ground." His soldier's instincts were coming back, fighting through the haze of pain-inspired confusion which was wrapped around his thoughts.

"Got to have the high ground." He didn't have numbers, he could still have position. He looked upslope and shook his head. There was no trail, no easy way up. The gray had stopped for a good reason—there was nowhere else to go.

"We'll have to find us a way. There's always a way," he said. If you can find it. It wasn't going to be easy. It took a hell of a long time to get aboard the sorrel. Three tries to find the stirrup with his boot toe, a long, long while to get the leg up and over. That tore the wound open again and Shell sat there drenched in his own sweat although the night was growing rapidly cold.

He started on, leading the gray.

The slope was littered with small rounded boulders, fist-sized to head-sized. The going was very bad. The sorrel slipped constantly, once going to a knee. There was no choice, Morgan swung down and led the horses onward.

It must have taken three hours to go a thousand feet. Maybe it just seemed like three hours, through the cactus, up that incline with his head throbbing, the horses balking, slipping. But when he finally reached the ledge the moon was rising and it had been rising late. Shell stood looking down the long dark slope to the desert flats, incredibly white in the moonlight. He couldn't make out the ruins of Chanticleer, could see no firelight, no lamplight anywhere in all the world.

Just the moon floating through a dark sky, chasing stars before it. Away off a coyote howled, mournfully, timelessly. Shell unsaddled the sorrel and just let the gear drop to the ground. He managed to get the hobbles on the horses' feet but after that he could do nothing else. He managed to get hold of his blanket and roll up in it before the lights went completely out and he lay there on the rocky ledge sunk deep into unconsciousness, the only refuge from the pain, the exhaustion.

The sunlight was in his eyes and Morgan couldn't figure that out. The sunlight was in his eyes and his body was on fire with fever.

He tried to rise and toppled over. Dragging himself on his hands and knees to his gear he disentangled the canteen and opened it with fumbling fingers, pouring the

115

water down his throat. He swallowed greedily, wiping at his lips with the back of his hand. He drank again and Shelter noticed his hand was shaking.

"It's bad," he told himself. Bad that the fever should have come on overnight, bad that he was still having trouble with his thoughts. The shock should have passed away. It hadn't.

He capped the canteen and dragged himself back to the edge of the precipice, the horses eyeing him uneasily.

Shell peered down the long slopes, spotting them almost immediately.

They were a long way off yet, but they were coming toward him, and by the way they rode it was obvious they had found his trail. That would be the Apache in the lead, and he would be a tracker.

"They're sure they've got me," Shell muttered. "I'm not so sure they're wrong," he added and then laughed bitterly. The laugh caused his back to ache again and he broke it off with a gasp of pain.

He sat sipping the water then, crossing his legs tailor-fashion. The sun was warm on his body, the ground beneath him warm. He had no wish to move just then. Looking above and behind him he could see the sharply rising cliff face studded with rocky outcroppings, and—higher up—shaded by a few gnarled, wind-flagged cedars. That was something—it might mean that there was water and grass somewhere up above. It might not.

One thing Morgan couldn't see was a way up. Nothing at all offered itself to his eyes as he searched the two-thousand foot bluff. Had there been a way he didn't feel up to it just then anyway. He hardly felt up to breathing in and breathing out, but that effort was necessary.

Eating was necessary as well. It was something else he

didn't feel up to, but his battered body needed nourishment. He sat there most of the morning on the rim of the outcropping, sipping water, eating from Yeats' food pack, watching the pursuit cross the plateau, watching the tiny dark dots take on color and form, become men on horseback.

Casually he counted them. Six, seven, eight, ten. That was a long way to split five-thousand dollars, but then they probably didn't intend on splitting it that far.

Shell reached out beside him and picked up the Winchester, slowly loading the magazine as the horsemen rode on behind the Apache. He knew it was the Apache. He could even make out the bandage on the man's arm.

"Wish to hell I'd finished you when I got your baldheaded partner," Shell said to himself.

He caught himself humming a little tune as he loaded the Winchester. He felt fine, fine as long as he didn't move, didn't try to rise. He wasn't going to have to move at all for this.

True, he was hot and his stomach was knotted, cramped, but it was no worse than having a touch of the ague. As long as you didn't move!

Then the little devils with their fiery pitchforks came back and jabbed at your back. The top of your skull would pop off and your brains would sit there throbbing . . . you couldn't move.

Shell had the Winchester full up, one in the chamber. He sat still, sipping the water, watching. They were nearly to him. He could make out Thornhill on his buckskin, the Campbells, the dark horse Jack Claypool rode, the yellow scarf around Claypool's neck.

He wanted them all, wanted them all dead.

It was a cool desire, not rage, hot and fiery, unreason-

117

ing. No, it was ice cold. These men were murderers who thought a few dollars was more important than a living breathing man. They quite simply didn't deserve to live.

Shell lifted his Winchester and sighted down the barrel, his finger slack beside the trigger guard. The horsemen were slowing to cross the rocky wash, the Apache still leading them. The Indian seemed to sense something. He glanced up and then lifted his hand, shouting out a warning. Maybe he had seen the sunlight on the barrel of the rifle, maybe he had just guessed it, but he began yelling, riding to one side. Shelter followed the horse with his sights and squeezed off. The Apache's pony rolled, throwing the Indian free. A ball of dust lifted from the plateau, marking the spot.

He switched his sights to another rider, one he couldn't make out at this distance. The Winchester recoiled against Shelter's shoulder and the man went down, blown from the saddle to lie motionless against the hard ground, a long, long way from home.

Shelter fired again—there was still no answering fire. They couldn't see a damn thing to shoot at. His bullet tagged Hector Campbell. Or was it Sam? Tough to tell them apart at this range, and the big man sagged forward. A mortal shot? Shelter was afraid not. He had hurried it as he now hurried the shot he sent pursuing the marshal of Jacumba who was riding hell for it toward the brushy draw to the east, riding low across his horse's neck, whipping the animal frantically with his hat.

Shell fired, missed, fired again and saw the marshal jerk upright in the saddle, slapping at his arm. Morgan wanted to shoot again but by then the marshal was into the brush, out of sight.

He switched his sights again. He got off a clean shot at a lagging outlaw and saw the man go down. Another pair of

118

shots were wasted at Jack Claypool—it had to be him—as he rode behind his horse's shoulder toward the ravine where the marshal had gone.

Shelter lowered the rifle from his shoulder and sat staring down at the plateau, thumbing fresh rounds into the Winchester.

"Two down for sure," he told himself. That meant it was only about eight to one now. The one, unfortunately, was on the brink of collapse. Some charge of adrenalin, some need to strike back had lifted him high enough for him to fight them off fairly successfully. Now he could feel the current slowly draining out of him, the pain returning as the fever, the headache continued to nag.

A man on a dark horse made a sudden dash from the ravine to the rocky gulley at the base of the bluff. Shelter fired twice, missed twice and sat watching the smoke curl from his gun, smelling the acrid powder smoke.

"They're coming after me," he told no one. It interested him distantly, like a mathematical problem. He was somewhat surprised that they had decided to come, but then he supposed they had to. They couldn't afford to let that gold get away from them, couldn't afford to let Shelter Morgan tell his tale of murder and treachery.

Another horseman rode from the ravine, his horse at a dead run, tail stretched out behind him, rider low across the withers. Shelter sighted, took a shallow breath and held it, squeezed off, and the rider went down. From the corner of his eye he saw another outlaw, but it was already too late to fire. He too had reached the bluff, and now there were two of them down there.

Shell inched forward, his side protesting, his skull aching, and he peered over the rim. A volley of shots racketed against the bluff, kicking up rock dust, whining off into space and Shelter withdrew hastily. They had him spotted now, and they were determined to protect the two men who were climbing the bluff.

And then there were three. Shell saw the pinto pony, knew it belonged to the Apache. He could see no rider— the Apache must have been tucked behind it as it ran. Shell sighted and then had to blink. His eyes refused to focus. Squinting down the sights he saw a row of black metal dots; the barrel of the rifle curved away bizarrely.

Opening his left eye didn't help. It seemed to double the confusion. He wiped angrily at his eyes with his shirt cuff, but by then the Apache had reached the bluff as well.

"This is no damned good," Shell muttered.

They would climb that bluff and they would have him. He couldn't lean out and shoot them off the cliff face with the other guns out there. The way his eyes were acting he wouldn't be able to shoot anyway.

"Up." He turned and looked up toward the rocky, broken peak behind him, toward where the gnarled cedar trees clung to the red-brown earth. "I've got to get up."

Just how in hell he was going to do it wasn't clear. He could barely walk, let alone climb, and he was damned if he could see any way to climb that peak. The horses, he had already decided, were to be abandoned. A man didn't last long out here without a horse; but if he didn't get off that ledge he just wasn't going to last at all.

Shell staggered to the pile of gear, snatched up the saddlebags with the gold and nearly buckled under their weight. He tossed it over his shoulder and hurriedly made a sling for his rifle from the gray's lead rope. Then he picked up the canteen and before he had time for second thoughts, he started up, up toward the high reaches while behind him the stalkers came.

11.

There was no way he was going to make it, but Shelter forced himself to believe he could, to believe he was in good shape for climbing, that there was nothing to scaling this molehill.

He wasn't real successful at that. The peak still stood jagged and sheer, and there was no way of making a molehill out of that mountain.

He began to climb because there was nothing else to do. To remain on that ledge was to die. There were three men below making their way up, protected by rifle fire from their friends in the draw.

Shelter worked his way up the cleft which was carved into the slope for a length of a hundred feet or so. It was good for starters, but a shelf broke out over it halfway up. Then there was nothing, just a series of untrustworthy toeholds, knobs of rock for handholds, bare rock where the brush which grew on the mountain could hardly penetrate. Plants tilted out crazily, bare roots exposed.

From far, far away something crackled and Shell reflexively pulled his head in tortoise-like. It wasn't necessary, that bullet was nowhere near him, but he had been spotted. There would be a mad rush now.

Shelter turned his head and glanced back. The rest of the outlaws had gotten to their horses and were storming toward the bluff. Shell didn't give them a moment's thought. They weren't the ones that bothered him. The ones on the bluff did. If they could get up onto the ledge soon enough they would have Shelter like a fish in a rain barrel. There he was pasted against the side of the peak, unable to even fight back.

The idea spurred him on.

He climbed, his back trickling blood, his head spinning, sweat dribbling into his eyes as the merciless sun beat down on his back.

He was moving slowly, far too slowly. He had to pause for long seconds to find a possible handhold, to test it before daring to put his weight on it and slowly, far too slowly, drag himself upward another few inches.

Looking up Shell could see a notch, and in the notch blue sky. That was to his left and some fifty feet up over broken ground where the mountain had crumbled. Above and beyond the notch was another pinnacle, unclimbable. To his right was a gentler grade leading into the highlands. That was where he wanted to be, but he just wasn't going to make it. He had to make the hard climb and he had to make it quickly.

Bowing his head briefly, feeling his muscles quiver, he started on, the gold tugging at his shoulder, pulling him down.

There was a shout below and Shelter clambered on, not looking back. The first shot rang off the stone ten feet or so above him. Rock rolled away from underfoot and he lost his grip, sliding back five feet, tearing the meat from his hands and knees.

Gritting his teeth he climbed on, able to hear the men below now.

"There he is! Get the lead out, damnit!"

"Morgan! Come down and we won't shoot."

Shell ignored the comedian, whoever he was, and climbed on, frantically, desperately. Shots ticked off the cliff all around now, spraying him with stone splinters, the ricochets whining past like angrily buzzing insects. Shell looked up and shook his head. He just wasn't going to make it.

"Damn you, get going, boy!" Morgan muttered to himself. "Going to hang here and die? Move it!"

He tried moving it. An inch at a time, it seemed, a painful inch at a time while bullets sprayed against the rock face. One of them was bound to get lucky sooner or later. It was a tricky shot upslope like that, but all of the odds were with them.

"Move!" The little voice fairly screamed and Morgan realized he had just been hanging there, clinging to a tentative fingerhold. Hanging, waiting to die. Well, damn them all, he wasn't ready to die yet. There was Joe Bass who had killed hundreds and lived to profit from it. There were other men who had killed their comrades down along the Conasauga, the bloody Conasauga, officers trusted to lead who had taken to their heels, betraying their soldiers, leaving them to suffer untold agonies. And there was no one, just no one to see that those men paid—except Shelter Morgan.

123

"Move!" It was too damned soon to die.

His fingers scraped rock, found a sudden handhold. Looking up he saw the narrow ledge, the notch above him. How he had made it he didn't know. But he had— almost. The rifles fired again and Shell gripped the ledge, rolling up and over, reaching the protection of the outcropping.

He lay there panting, his heart leaping in and out of his throat as his back spasmed with ugly pain. It seemed hours before he could move, but he knew he had to. He looked up to the high notch, wondering.

He didn't know this country. It was possible there was a way around, a way Thornhill or the Apache would know. He had to move on though, he couldn't stay here.

Cautiously he crept to the edge of the outcropping and looking down the chute he could see two men, rifles slung on their backs, making the climb. But they were coming much faster than Shelter had.

He looked to the right and then the left, seeing the stack of crumbling boulders tilted against the red shoulder of the mountain.

Shell got behind it and pushed. It took surprisingly little effort. The rocks broke free, bounded away and went racketing down the long chute.

A scream of terror met Shell's ears. When he looked over the rim again there was one man upright standing over two crooked figures. They had fallen a long way and then been hit by the boulders, tough. Morgan couldn't dredge up a lot of sympathy. It was easy to remember what those men had come out on the desert for.

Shell stood on wobbly legs looking up toward the notch in the hills. He picked up his rifle and the saddlebags and started on, walking into the wilderness mountain range, not knowing where he was going, knowing only that there were thunder guns behind him.

He stumbled over the boulders and broken shale, walking toward the notch where the sunlight shone like some beacon of promise. It was hot, airless in the shadow of the peak. His legs began to betray him. He would take three, six, a dozen steps and then suddenly the knees would give. He fell twice, the second time banging his shoulder painfully against a rock.

He lay there, his back opening up again and the pain was overpowering enough to wring tears of frustration from his eyes as the little men with the sledge hammers pounded away at his skull.

"Get up, damn you," he growled, and he actually made it to his feet, stumbling on.

Somehow he made it to the notch and he stood there numbed, looking down the far side. There was no way down!

The land simply fell away. To his left was a high rising peak, and beyond that many more rugged mountains. To his left the rounded, tilted shoulder of mountain separated from the rest of the range by the narrow notch, and beyond that the bluff.

Directly before him was a thousand feet of littered slope so sheer that a mountain goat would have detoured around it. Nothing grew there, nothing could apparently. Thousands of small rocks dusted the chocolate-colored slope—all of them appeared ready to move at the slightest whim of gravity, the tiniest nudge from wind or rain or the trembling earth.

Shell stood there, the dry wind raking his body, tugging at his shirt as it gusted up the long slope. There was no going back, not with the guns back there. It was forward or sit down and die.

He started down the slope, the saddlebags across one shoulder, the rifle across the other. He moved cautiously, going to his rump to scoot ahead painfully, slowly, foolishly. He was on the ragged edge here. He couldn't risk standing up. Once a man lost his balance he would be gone. If Shell began to fall he would fall the length of the slope.

The wind hurled insults at him, jabbed at him with dry, dusty fingers. Shell worked his way northward, taking it as quickly as possible. Behind him they would be coming. There would be a deal of caution in them now, but they would come on all the same.

He didn't look down any more than he had to, just ahead and to his right where the chalky hills, out of place among all the dark colored mountains, poked their heads skyward.

The land was flatter there, there were trees to be seen. Once Shell saw the silver glint of sunlight on something reflective. Water? It was possible. He didn't think about water much now, didn't think about his fever or the debilitating pain in his back. He thought about those hills, those chalky hills, beautiful hills where a man would actually be able to stand up, to walk beneath the trees.

It was growing darker on the eastern slopes now and Shelter went on with a kind of panic. To be caught on that slope after dark would be deadly. With each movement he kicked a rock or two free and he could see them bound away into the maw of the canyon. His body would do roughly the same thing.

The wind was very still. The sky was crimson fire above the dark peaks. Far away a patch of white sand desert became a pinkish lake. And Shelter Morgan stood beside the pine tree watching it all.

He was drenched in sweat. His legs would barely support him. But he was there, there in the white hills, standing on his own two feet.

But he hadn't beaten them—not just yet. He was sick to death, so weak he could barely support himself, out of water, food, hatless, horseless, with no idea in the world which way he was going or what he expected to find once he got there.

He started on because that was all there was to do. You keep moving or they come and bury you.

He took a dozen steps before he fell. It was minutes, hours? before he rose again and started on.

"You can't have me, damnit!" he hissed. They weren't going to find him down. You've got to move or they bury you. He made only three more steps before the bottom of the world fell out and he was tumbling through a dark and endless space, falling, falling until someone pulled the dark curtains shut and there was nothing any more.

He was swimming in a river of blood and there were others in it with him, their skull-like faces bobbing by. Men he knew, men from a long while back. Men he had killed. Grinning, accusing, screaming skulls floating on the bloody river.

Shell woke up in a sweat. He woke up and the agony came with consciousness. Pain, terrible pain grinding at his brain. He couldn't see. That scared him, really scared him. He was blind, and God, he didn't want to be blind. They would find him and if he was blind he couldn't fight back. He stared at the blackness for a long while and eventually he saw it. The most beautiful thing in creation, a tiny silver star winking at him from out of the depths of the surrounding blackness.

"Not blind—it's just black as sin," Shelter muttered. "Got to get up."

That wasn't so damned easy. He was twisted around and wedged into something. His back flared with pain as he tried to move to discover what had happened. Rocks. He was lying among some rocks. He must have stumbled over a ledge in the darkness.

Now what? "Now what, get up, you dumb bastard!" But he couldn't get up and when he tried it the pain nearly split him open and he went out again, falling into the endless night.

The dreams got stranger.

He was riding a two-headed horse across the sand dunes. The horse sank into the coppery sand and the tentacles clutched at him as the *things* rose up. Of course—the sand dunes were under water; but the horse was gone and the dolphins were no help at all.

And then the woman came. Soft and lovely, beautiful, her hair scented, clean, glossy, her eyes large and dark, her hands gentle as they moved across his flesh. Shell's eyes flickered open. The evening breeze had grown cool. Her hands were still soft as she hunched over him, trying to free him from the rocks.

"God damn, Shelter Morgan!" Kolka said and he lay back smiling, knowing he wasn't dreaming any longer.

12.

It was cool and dark in the cave. Beyond the mouth of the cave was clear blue sunlight. Shelter Morgan lay looking at the sunlight and shadow for a long while, trying to make some sense out of it.

There had been a woman. A long run, a lot of shots fired and then a woman.

"What woman?" He yawned as he asked himself. He looked around, not seeing much in the dim cavern interior. He was lying on a bed of pine boughs, he could tell that by the scent. It was a springy, rather comfortable bed. He was on his stomach for some reason. A slight movement told him the reason as a pain shot through his lower back.

The pain brought awareness back. He recalled it all suddenly. The five thousand, the treachery of the marshal, the long climb and the short fall. The woman . . .

"Kolka," Shell said out loud.

"God damn!" she said and Shell laughed out loud. She had been sitting in the shadows, and now she rose to walk to him, to hunker down and tilt her head, to peer into his eyes.

"I'm all right," Shell said.

There was no answer. Kolka touched his forehead, her hand was cool and competent. Shell's weapons, the saddlebags had been placed near at hand. Kolka indicated them, scooting the Colt nearer. She was a wise woman for one so young, knowing that Morgan needed that security right now with the killers on his backtrail.

She went away for a while and then came back with a bowl of rabbit stew. Shelter tried to sit up, couldn't quite make it and had to be satisfied with being spoonfed.

It was good, very good, and it was nice having Kolka close by taking care of him. He tried to talk to her but it wasn't much use.

"Where's your grandfather, Kolka? Old man? Did something happen to him? How long have I been out anyway? How long sleep?" She spooned another mouthful of stew up. "I don't want to eat any more. It was good, I was hungry, but I don't want to eat now."

"Eat." She mulled that over. She must have heard the word before. "Eat." She said it in a voice of command and Shelter surrendered to her edict just to assure her that "eat" meant eat.

"No more," he said a while later. "It's too much. I'm full. Big belly!" he grinned. Kolka didn't grin in return.

"Eat!"

"No."

"God damn, Shelter Morgan." She rose and flounced away to the far corner, and Shelter watched her, liking the swing and sway of her hips beneath the cotton skirt she wore.

She squatted down and began doing whatever she had been doing before. Her fingers were busy, her eyes intent on her work.

"Kolka?"

She refused to look up. The fingers continued to work away. She seemed to be sewing beads onto a buckskin shirt.

"Hey!" Shell shouted, but still she ignored him.

He sighed and lay back down, but he had had enough sleep, and it was no good trying to doze. There were too many things he had to know, had to do.

Where was he and where was the Thornhill-Campbell gang? When and where was the ransom supposed to be paid to Joe Bass? Was the girl even alive? He wasn't getting any answers lying there but when he tried to sit up the pain knifed through him again. His head started reeling. He sagged back and then had to lie down again, shifting to his back. He needed a new position of some sort, even if this did press his wound against the bed causing some discomfort. The aching spine and muscles demanded some change.

Kolka had begun to watch him suddenly, watch the slow progress, the collapse, the shifting of position. Now as Shell lay on his back, winded by the small exertion she turned her eyes away, back to her work again.

"I suppose that was amusing to you," Shell said sharply. "Ah, hell, what am I bothering to talk to you for . . . maybe the old man will be back soon."

But he wasn't there at supper time. Or what Kolka had decided would be supper time. Outside the sky was coloring, going to soft purple and deep blue. Night wasn't far

131

off—another day wasted, and Shell could only curse his useless, stoved-up body.

Kolka came to him, tasting the stew with her finger. She knelt down near his head and propped him up on her knees, feeding him slowly, deftly.

Between bites Shell tried again to communicate with the Kikima woman.

"Where is your grandfather?"

Bite. Chew and swallow, sonny. Kolka was going to continue with her nursing come hell or high water.

"How long did I sleep?"

Bite.

"Where is Hanapa?" The old man's name suddenly came back to Shelter and as he used it for the first time he touched some responsive chord in the girl's mind.

"Hanapa," she repeated and then started babbling away so quickly that Morgan couldn't have followed if he did know the Kikima language, which he didn't.

"Tell me again, darlin'," Shell said, reaching up to place a finger on her lips. He let it linger there and then touched his own ear. "Slower. I don't understand."

"Hanapa," she repeated and then she crossed her hands together in front of her.

"They've got him captive?" Shell crossed his own wrists as if they were tied. "Someone has got Hanapa and is holding him captive?"

Shell looped an imaginary rope around Kolka's wrists and held them together, looking at her questioningly. "Like that. Someone has captured Hanapa?"

She shook her head vigorously, dropping her spoon in her excitement, She began to chatter again, crossing her wrists, pointing at Shelter, at his guns until it sunk in.

Someone had Hanapa and Shelter Morgan was going to

132

make him free with his guns. The thought was too absurd to laugh at. She saw the look in his eyes and moved away, hurt and broken-hearted.

"I just can't do it, girl. I can't fight now. Don't you see?"

She didn't see. She stood with her back to him, her head hanging as dusk pooled against the cavern floor and the torch of the sun flickered and died against the desert sky.

Fight, hell, he could hardly walk. And when he was able to get up and do something he was going after Joe Bass. There was Dorothy Patch to worry about and then Joe Bass himself to have a little talk with. If there was any time for a sideshow he might want to look up Marshal Thornhill. There just wasn't time to get involved in some Indian trouble.

"Once a friend, always a friend," the old man had said. But Morgan hardly knew him. Still it wasn't a good feeling to turn down the girl and as he lay there staring at the cavern ceiling he muttered, "The hell with it. All right! Where is he? Where's Hanapa?"

The girl didn't answer. She didn't understand any of what he said—great, that made her an efficient ally. Well, maybe she could hold him up while he fought . . . she was there and her body was smooth, naked, whispering against Shell's flesh in the night.

There was a faint glow outside, a rosy hue, fading rapidly to darkness but by it for one moment Shell could see her silhouette, the jouncing, pert breasts, the sleek hips, long thighs, rounded buttocks. Then he could feel her against him, feel her snuggle in, her hands taking their time as they roamed down across his chest to his abdomen, dropping to his groin to test and heft Shell, to

133

feel the slowly pulsing, slowly growing erection, the tightening of his sack.

She bent low and her loose hair grazed his flesh as she kissed him on the inner thigh, her lips inflaming him.

He couldn't move much, didn't dare to with that wound in his back. He stretched out his hands and rested them on the smooth expanse of her buttocks, feeling the taut skin stretched over feminine muscle.

Her hands had now encircled his erection and she sat back, tossing her hair over her shoulder, toying with him, her fingers slow and sure, tugging at him.

Shell's hand slid up her thigh to find the warmth hidden in the soft bush which flourished between her sleek legs. A finger dipped inside of her soft dampness and she quivered a little, lifting one leg, allowing him access to stroke her gently from side to side, in and out, working around the tautening, sensitive tab of flesh which yearned to be manipulated.

"God damn," she said abruptly, switching position.

She turned, straddled him, facing Shell, and gripping his shaft slowly lowered herself. Her eyes were bright—a thin sliver of starlight from outside caught the intense concentration on her face and lighted it. Shell simply lay back, watching the woman squat slowly on him, feeling the warmth of her take him in, feeling the steady, needful pulsing begin in his loins.

Kolka hovered over him, her hand holding his erection as she swiveled herself on the head of it, slowly stroking herself, drawing it up and out to touch her clitoris before settling again, deeply, urgently, a small rush of fluid inside her escaping to lubricate the soft, expanding muscle.

Shell's hands lifted to her breasts. He toyed with the

dark, taut nipples there and she shuddered. His left hand continued to caress her breasts, one then the other, and his right hand dropped to her crotch to find her fingers, to intertwine with them as she touched his shaft and buried him deep within her.

Her fingers were slippery, busy, intent, and she clutched at Shell's hand with them as she grabbed at his erection.

Shell tried to move but couldn't, his back forced him to lie still and he did so now, lying back with his eyes closed, his hands behind his head, all of his concentration on the one warm, fluid spot where they joined, where Kolka lifted and lowered her body, working against him, finding the spot she had been looking for, rubbing herself excitedly against him in a frantic sideways motion until with a small muffled shriek she gave way to a trembling orgasm as Shelter, no longer able to hold back, no longer wanting to, met her climax with his own.

He lay back in the night, stroking her thighs, back, buttocks, and she tumbled forward, her dark hair falling across his face and shoulders, utterly spent.

They lay together, hearts slowing their wild pace, and Shell pulled the thin blanket up over both of them. He was nearly asleep, vastly content, when he heard her whisper, or thought he heard, "God damn, Shelter Morgan."

With the dawn he was up and dressing. A series of slow, stiff, painful movements. Getting his pants on was incredibly drawn-out, even with Kolka helping, holding onto the vitals while he eased his jeans up over his hips, her hands getting things settled.

His shirt was a rag. There was a spare, maroon shirt in Yeats' saddlebags, an inch or two too short in the cuffs, and inch or two too small in the chest, but it was an improvement anyway.

He finally got his boots on, his Colt buckled and he was, as far as being clad goes, ready. But ready for battle? No. Not hardly.

They ate again, more rabbit stew and Shelter tried desperately to communicate with Kolka, to find out what the old man's situation was, where he was, who had him, why.

"Kolka," he said, taking her hands, looking seriously into her eyes. "Hanapa is a prisoner." Again the crossing of wrists to indicate a bound man.

"Yes." She knew that much now. Shelter had taught her yes and no. That, however, was the limit of her knowledge. The rest was sign language.

"Where is he? Where is Hanapa?" There was no answer. She only cocked her head in a birdlike manner, standing looking at him.

He took her hand and walked her to the mouth of the cave. Below, tangled, dry mountains stretched out for jumbled miles. The daylight was piercing after the time in the cave. Shell pointed toward the north.

"Hanapa?"

"No." She grabbed his arm and shifted it north by west. "Hanapa."

"How far?"

She shrugged again. Damn it all. There was no way around it—she was going to have to go along, lead him to Hanapa and hope that she didn't get herself killed.

"Who took him, Kolka?" There was no answer, just that same tilted head, those same interested, bright eyes. Shell held up two fingers behind his head. "Indians?"

"No." She laughed. Holding up two fingers of her own

she took them in the other hand and covered them. "White men then." Shell frowned. Who else was in these hills? Joe Bass and the Thornhill gang. Was it possible that the marshal was holding Hanapa hostage to use against Shell—no, he couldn't know that Morgan knew the old man or cared what happened to him.

They tried a little more communication, but it just wasn't getting them anywhere. The way to find out was to go have a look-see. They started half an hour later, Kolka carrying the saddlebags with the ransom money over her shoulders, her camp sack—knife, salt, jerky, flour—in her hand. Shell was travelling light with the Colt on his hip, the Winchester slung over his shoulder. He had asked Kolka about horses, but she had seen none. That gray apparently was gone for good. Too bad, he favored that pony.

They walked most of the morning toward the northwest, halting during the heat of the early afternoon to rest. Shelter needed it, needed it badly.

"I'm getting damned discouraged, Kolka. This body of mine seems to be letting me down a lot lately. A little blood leaks out and first thing you know it doesn't want to do anything. I get dizzy, tired, well there's not much point talking to you about it, is there?"

Maybe. Maybe not. She didn't understand a word of it, but she listened, she cared that he was trying to communicate with her, to share something, whatever it was.

Shell drew her near and kissed her forehead. He held her hand for a minute, looking into those black, questioning eyes. Then with a glance at the sun he rose.

"We'd better keep moving."

They started on, up the long rock canyons, Shelter's breathing labored as his deprived muscles fought to

137

handle the slopes. Once they had crested the ridge they moved along faster, following the skyline. Beyond them the mountains tangled together. Far below the desert lay placid and broad, white in the sunlight. Kolka began to move more rapidly now. There was excitement in her eyes.

"Are we getting near?" Shell asked, his voice dry.

Kolka turned back, her finger to her lips. They were near then, very near, and fifteen minutes later Shelter saw the camp.

There it was, in a small valley where patchy grass grew. There were half a dozen horses grazing on the grass, and beyond the horses was a canvas tent, like an old army tent. Shelter looked around, seeing the rising chalky cliffs, the dark peak beyond. A winking silver thread stretched down the mountain, showing the path of a tiny rill.

"Joe Bass." It had to be Bass' hideout. There was no reason for anyone else to be hidden out in such a desolate spot.

Kolka touched her finger to his lips and Shell nodded. She was right. Their voices would carry down that long canyon and although it was most of a mile to where the little tent was pitched, in the desert stillness that was near enough.

Shelter looked over the camp for a long while, seeing nothing, no one, although there had to be someone down there watching the horses.

Kolka tapped his shoulder and they moved out, scrambling down a dusty slope, climbing a narrow hogback beyond. When they topped it they were right above the camp. Shell could have spit and hit it. He could have spit and hit the guard who was crouched in the rocks

138

below them.

Shell froze, only his eyes moving. Down the white bluff there was one man, then the dry grass and the horses. Then the little tent and what had to be a fire ring. Beyond that the pines began to grow, tall, dry-looking trees, growing denser as they straggled up the dark peak beyond the camp.

Shell scooted back over the hogback and sat there, looking at Kolka. With his finger he drew a plan of the camp in the dust. Tent, trees, meadow, cliffs.

"Hanapa?" he asked, lifting his eyes and the girl pointed to the woods beyond the tent.

"Then there's only one way to get him, isn't there?" Shell said beneath his breath. Go on down and snatch him. Snatch him away from five or six armed men. And the girl, Dorothy Patch, was she down there too? Or already dead, perhaps.

Shelter sat there for a while on the dry slope, the wind blowing over him, lifting his dark hair. He had felt inadequate at times, but this one was nearly a topper.

One wounded man and a squaw against an outlaw gang. He couldn't move fast and he couldn't fight hard. If there was real trouble he couldn't run away from it, and if he blew this he just might be ending the lives of an old man and two women.

He had no cards.

"Wait till dark," Morgan said, "and we'll have at it."

13.

Dusk was in the desert mountains and the camp below came to life with firelight and men moving to their supper. Shelter lay there atop the hogback counting heads, watching the sentries as he had been throughout the afternoon.

There were five men visible now—that left two horses unaccounted for. They could be spares or there could be two more people somewhere. One of them Dorothy Patch? Shell wondered how the old man was holding up. His heart didn't appear to be very good and John Patch was having a rough time of it. His only son gone bad, his only daughter abducted.

With luck, with a lot of luck, Shelter had a chance at putting that right. The ransom money was his only edge, his only hole card. If Randy Patch, alias Joe Bass, wanted that money bad enough he would play the game Shelter's way. That Shelter held in reserve. If he could he was going to return that money to a sick old man who probably needed it.

And with it a daughter.

"You stay here, you hear me?" Shell said sternly. The shadows were growing deep, blending, merging, the darkness of night settling over the hills.

Kolka knew what he was telling her all right, but she pretended she didn't. When Shell got up to go, she made a move to join him.

"No." He held her wrists tightly in the darkness. "You stay here. I mean it."

Then, hefting the saddlebags he started off along the hogback, staying behind the ridge, below the skyline. A quarter of a mile on when it was nearly full dark, he stopped, placed the saddlebags in a narrow crevice and kicked crumbled stone in over them, hiding the gold.

He paused in the darkness, looking ahead and then back. Damn her! He couldn't see Kolka, couldn't hear her, but he sensed her presence somehow. She was following, coming to *help*. And it would be a real help if they caught her, wouldn't it?

Shell couldn't do much about it now, however; and so he moved on, feeling his way along the slope, from time to time rising up to look toward the campfire below him, taking his bearings.

He had left the rifle with Kolka, so he had both hands free to climb with. The Winchester wasn't going to do him much good on a job like this anyway. It had to be silent, quick and absolutely silent.

Hanapa could be counted upon to act silently, swiftly—if he wasn't hurt. The girl was a different story. But then Shell was thinking too far ahead again; who said

141

that the girl was down there, alive?

Morgan was nearly into the timber now, and the hog-back flattened out, merging with the dark hills beyond. Shell circled on, keeping the fire in sight through the trees.

He went suddenly flat, pressing himself against the pine-needle-littered earth. A sentry had appeared directly before Shell. A tall man with a rifle, his shadow separating itself from the surrounding forest, a sudden, menacing figure.

The guard wasn't looking that way, however. He hadn't seen Shelter or heard him. It was a wonder. Morgan's body was moving clumsily. His reactions were slow, awfully slow.

But this guard was no woodsman, no rough country soldier, and Shelter knew he had him. He had only to lie still, to wait . . .

When the guard was past him, behind the big pine, Shelter got to his feet, moving with slow stealth. He walked forward, drawing his Colt as he went, creeping behind the guard like a shadow at his heels.

The guard's head started to turn and Shelter's hand fell. The Colt thunked off the side of the Bass man's skull, above the ear, dropping him in a heap at Shelter's feet.

One down. Shelter bent low and picked up the guard's rifle, slipping his sidearm from his holster. The pistol Shell jammed in behind his waistband, the rifle he heaved away after ejecting the cartridges.

Then he moved on through the dark, dark pines. Their scent was heavy in his nostrils as was the dust of the camp. He was nearly at the perimeter of the trees now and he slowed his pace, circling south again, moving toward the position Kolka had indicated.

There were three men around the red campfire out in the clearing. One in the tent? He had seen the canvas flutter lightly once, but that might have been a vagrant breeze. It could also be the girl—if she was in the tent, she was going to be tough to get at, very tough indeed.

Shell pulled up short, stepped behind a tree and stood trying to hold his breath, to still his heart. He had nearly stepped on another guard. The man was sitting on the ground, rifle across his lap, plate in his hands, eating.

And across the small clearing from him sat Hanapa tied to a tree.

Slowly Shelter surveyed the area, seeing no one else. When his eyes went past Hanapa, the old man's head came up, he looked left and then right, searching. He knew.

The man with the tin plate full of beans didn't know anything. He didn't get long to think about it. Shell stepped forward, slammed his Colt against the base of his skull and rolled the unconscious man into the trees.

Six long strides then with his heart thumping and he was to Hanapa, cutting him loose.

The old man didn't say a word until Shell bent down and asked, "Where is the girl, Hanapa? Is there a girl in this camp?"

"Kolka?" The old man was rubbing his wrists.

"Kolka's fine. She brought me here. Answer me, old man—is there a white woman in this camp?"

"Yes, yes, Shelter Morgan. In the tent. Have you a gun for me?"

Shelter offered him a rifle and a pistol. The Kikima Indian took the rifle without hesitation.

"You get on out of here now, Hanapa. Kolka's up on the high ridge, waiting."

"I will not go. Is your job finished?"

"Not yet, but it's my job, not yours," Shelter whispered savagely.

"No. You need help."

"I don't need you getting yourself killed or captured again."

"I will help." Hanapa answered resolutely.

"You're too old."

"Too old?" Hanapa smiled. "We shall see one day. We will run a race, you and I."

"All right." There really wasn't time to argue. If the old man wanted to risk it, Shell wasn't going to stop him. He couldn't, it seemed, and despite what he had told Hanapa, he knew that the old Indian was a match for him in almost anything but raw strength. His agility just now had to be far superior. The wound had opened up with all the climbing and running and blood was leaking down Shell's hip again. That angered him, oddly. It just plain angered him that someone had punched a hole through the fairly efficient machine that was his body.

"What do we do, Morgan?"

"I think the horses, don't you?"

"Yes," Hanapa answered with a delighted little smile, a toothless smile. "The horses first. I have always gone for the horses first in my raids."

"That's what we'll do then, and I'll leave that to you. Can you get to the other side of the meadow and get that string of ponies?"

"Yes. Of course. They will not see me nor hear me. I am a shadow on the night breeze . . ."

"Sure," Shell said, cutting him off before Hanapa could get real wound-up. "Get those damned horses. Keep them all if you can handle them; if not, scatter them as well as possible. Make plenty of noise once you're free, okay?"

"I will fire the gun many times."

"Right. On the first shot I'll move toward the tent and try getting the girl out of there."

"Be careful, Shelter Morgan. The man, he sleeps in there with her."

"What man?"

"The young man. Bass, they call him. I heard that name many times. Joe Bass."

"All right," Shell said, resting a hand briefly on the old man's narrow shoulder. "Move off then. Do me a favor and keep your head down. Kolka wouldn't forgive me if anything happened to you. If I can, I'll meet you south of here, in the small canyon." Shell had spotted that from the hogback, and the old man knew where it was apparently. He agreed. "You be careful," Shell added.

"It is battle, my friend. Battle! There is no other way to die if a man must die."

Hanapa nodded and then was gone, moving off on soft, noiseless feet toward the meadow while Shelter hunkered down to wait.

Battle. Hanapa said there was no other way to die for a man. Shell thought he could come up with a few. He wanted to go in bed when his time came, peacefully, after finishing with a ravishing woman. The odds were it would never come to that. Morgan had chosen battle as a way of life and it would be his own body that was left on the field one of these times. Had to be.

His eyes shifted to the tent. Nothing seemed to be happening out there. The men at the campfire beyond the tent were still eating. Would one of them soon be coming to relieve the unconscious man in the woods?

145

How much time was there; where was Hanapa? He just wasn't as young as both of them pretended.

Again Shell looked at the tent, counting the steps to reach it, the retreat which would have to be to the south, toward the gulley beyond the fallen pine.

So Joe Bass was sleeping in there, was he? Was it just that he wanted to keep an eye on the girl or did young Joe Bass get other ideas? Shell recalled the picture of the blonde on the old man's lap. She was a hell of a fine looking woman, was Dorothy Patch.

The shot rang out and Shelter came out of his crouch like a rising panther. The horses were running, raising a cloud of dust as they pounded eastward, toward the canyon mouth.

"What the hell . . . !" someone shouted from near the fire.

"The horses. They've got the horses."

"Who?"

"Damnit, run! If they get to the pass, we'll be walking out of this desert."

Tin plates and cups flew everywhere and the cowboys took off, running awkwardly in their high heeled boots. But running wasn't something they did much of, and they weren't going to catch any horses that way.

There was a spate of gunfire from near the horses, Hanapa filling the air with harmless lead. A few wild shots from the Bass gang chased night shadows in the sky.

Shelter sucked up a deep breath and made his move. He darted toward the tent, moving softly, his Colt held before him, eyes searching the darkness. There seemed to be no one around, just no one. He was ten steps from the tent when there suddenly was someone.

146

A man, a young man, stepped from the tent, looked first toward the stampede and then back toward the rushing footsteps behind him. He swiveled, clawing at his holster, trying to bring up his handgun. Finally it slipped free of the holster and the kid squeezed off.

Shelter was already hurtling through the air, and now as the shot blazed a trail over his shoulder and into the timber, Morgan's shoulder piled into the ribcage of the outlaw, driving the breath from him, slamming him to the ground with Shell on top of him.

"Damn you," the kid muttered and he tried to bring the pistol to bear, but Morgan had the Colt by the barrel and he twisted out and back, hard. It was let go or lose a forefinger and the kid let go.

Shelter winged the Colt aside and got to his feet, yanking the outlaw up to face him. He looked across the badman's shoulder once, that shot could have summoned help, but no one seemed to be coming yet. The horses held their attention.

"Where is she?" Morgan asked.

"Where's who?" The kid was slim, dark-haired, with a straight nose, slightly pointed chin, an almost girlish mouth which nevertheless showed a certain inner strength.

"The girl, damn you!" Shelter was in no mood for game-playing. He lifted the kid to tiptoes and shook him violently. "Where in the hell is she?"

"Why, I'm right here," the soft voice from behind Morgan said. It was soft, all right, feminine, but there was something deadly in the tone. He turned very slowly, still holding the kid by the shirt collar.

"Dorothy Patch?"

"That's right, sir," she replied. There was something

147

big and deadly in her hands. Morgan was looking right down the muzzle of a .44 revolver, looking death right in the damned eye. "I'm Dorothy Patch and if you don't let go of my man there, I'm very afraid I'll have to blow a hole right through you."

The kid was grinning, and as Shell slowly released his grip on his collar the grin got larger.

"You'd better let me have that for safe keeping," the kid said, tearing the Colt out of Shelter's hand. Then he stepped back to stand beside the girl, both of them with their pistols leveled on Shell's belly.

Even then Morgan might have made a try—why not, they were going to kill him—but two of the outlaw band came back from the futile pursuit of the horses.

"No luck, Joe. They're long gone . . . who the hell's that?" the outlaw asked in astonishment.

"I don't know, but I intend to find out," the kid said.

"First the Indian then this son of a bitch. I don't like this, Joe. Not when we're afoot. Say—" eyes shifted to Shelter. "This Yahoo's got something to do with those horses being snatched. Where the hell are they, friend?"

The man had a Texas accent, a tight unsmiling mouth, small eyes which shined in the campfire light. He stepped nearer to Shell, his rifle held menacingly.

Without additional warning the outlaw thumped the stock of his rifle against Shell's belly, thumped it hard and Shell buckled, nearly going to his knees. The Texan came a step nearer and thumped him again.

"Where are those damned horses?"

"Take it easy, Ned," the kid said.

"Take it easy!" the Texan exploded. "You know what kind of position we're in out here now? Ask this sucker here. They're close around, aren't they? Damned close."

148

"Who?" Shelter asked mildly.

"Who!" The rifle thumped again, the butt of the stock digging into Shell's body, the pain going all the way through to dig at his wounded back.

Morgan wasn't going to take any more. He just wasn't. He grabbed the rifle with both hands and kicked out, his bootheel landing solidly on the badman's kneecap. He wrenched the rifle free and pulled away and then from the corner of his eye he saw the flash of movement, recognized it for what it was—a hand with a pistol in it. Then he recognized nothing else, knew nothing else.

There was a sharp ringing like iron against iron far back in his skull, then some faceless angel decided to take him on a rapid trip of the star-strung universe where comets exploded in vivid colors, breathing hot fire on Shell's face.

When he came around he was sitting in the small tent, propped against a wooden crate. He opened one eye and winced with the pain. He could see shadowy figures standing over him but he didn't want to make the effort to focus on them, to identify them.

"Joe Bass?" Shell guessed.

"That's right," the kid answered.

Then Shell did open an eye. There was the slender kid, behind him the Texan looking self-satisfied. The girl was gone. "Where's the marshal?" Joe Bass asked.

"Go to hell," Shelter said.

"I'm asking you politely. Where's the damned marshal?"

"I'm telling you politely. Go to hell, Bass."

The Texan stepped around Bass and for a minute Shell thought he was going to take another trip through the starry universe, but Bass held the man back.

149

"Easy, Ned. That's not going to get us anywhere."

"That's right, Ned," Shell answered a little sarcastically. "Unconscious men don't talk very well."

"But you're not going to talk anyway. That's it, isn't it?" Joe Bass said.

"Now you've got it."

"All right." Bass turned away with a heavy, impatient shrug. "I've got to know what's happening. I've got to know where my horses are, where Thornhill is, how many men he has. You understand that."

"Sure."

"And you're going to talk. Do you understand that?" Joe Bass bent over at the waist, peering down into those cold blue eyes of Morgan. "You are going to talk one way or the other."

Shell was ready to tell him to stuff it again. He didn't get the chance. The tent flap opened and another strong arm boy came in. He shoved her forward and she hit the ground hard. Morgan ground his teeth together in frustration. Kolka just looked up at him, her shame showing.

She knew what he was talking about when he whispered, "Damn you, Kolka. Damn you, woman. I told you to stay put."

14.

She lay there small and beautiful, crumpled against the ground. Morgan sighed and took a step toward her. Ned, the Texan, tried to block his way, but Shell elbowed past, reaching the girl. He took her wrists, pulled and set her on her feet.

"I found her on the hogback," one of the men said.

"And what in the hell does she want? You, girl!" Bass said loudly. "What do you want here?"

"She doesn't speak English," Morgan said.

"No?" Bass spun on Shelter. "Well, you sure as hell do, and I'm going to have some answers out of you."

Dorothy Patch had returned. She was wearing a man's shirt, a pair of jeans and a flat-brimmed hat. She slipped into the tent and stood, arms folded, watching and listening.

"What are you after anyway?" Bass asked. "The three

of you. First we catch the old man spying on us, then you show up. Now the girl."

"Simple. The old man's the girl's grandfather. She and I came after him. He wasn't spying on you, Bass. He doesn't work for Thornhill and neither do I."

"You don't do you?" Bass said angrily.

"No."

"Who do you work for? You're not a lawman."

"No."

"I thought not." Bass paced the tent. "You rode out with Thornhill and you decided to track me yourself. There must be some kind of a reward posted by now. How much?"

"A thousand," Shell said.

"I thought so. Didn't want to split it, did you?"

"I'm not interested in the money," Morgan said.

"No, of course not," Joe Bass said with a harsh laugh. "No one is interested in money. Mind telling me what you are doing out here, Morgan?"

"I wanted to talk to you."

"Now we've had our chat. I didn't learn a hell of a lot though." Bass was rolling a smoke; now he jammed it into his mouth and lit it, blinking through the smoke. "What do I do with you now, Morgan? Just what can I do with you and the girl?"

"You'll let us go. The girl right now," Shell said quietly.

"The hell—so you can run back to Thornhill and tell him where we are?"

"No. I have reasons for not wanting to see the marshal again. You don't have to worry about that. But you've got to let the girl go or none of this will be worth a damn for you."

Bass' eyes narrowed. "What are you talking about?"

"I've got the ransom."

"What!" Bass jerked upright, the cigarette falling from his lips. "The hell you do!"

"The hell I don't. Five thousand gold dollars. The banker, Yeats, was carrying it until Yeats got shot down."

"Shot down by who?"

"I don't know. Someone who was working with Thornhill, the Campbells and Jack Claypool."

"He don't have the ransom, Joe," Ned said.

"Shut up!" Bass ran a hand across his forehead. "The Campbells and Claypool—God, they really want me dead, don't they?"

"That seemed to be the idea."

"And Dorothy?"

"What?" That threw Shell.

"What are they going to do with Dorothy?"

"Take her home, I guess." Shelter looked at the blonde. She returned his glance spitefully.

"Joe, we've got to find those horses or leg it out of here now," Ned insisted.

Bass ignored him. "The gold. Where is it?"

"Uh-uh. Not until you let the girl go."

"I'll still have you."

"That's right," Morgan said, "you'll still have me."

"The gold isn't going to do us a bit of good without the horses," Ned said.

"What do you know about the horses, Morgan?"

"Who says I know anything about them?"

"You do. There's no one else around but you and the Indians. You fixed this up as a diversion so that you could sneak in here and snatch Dorothy away."

"Did I?"

"Yes, damn you!" Joe Bass came a step nearer, his fists bunching. He was wading in deep water now and he knew it. Without ponies and money he was a dead man. Shelter Morgan was the key to both of those. He had to make a deal or toss in his cards.

"Well?" Shell prompted. "Time might be getting short. Thornhill can't be far off."

Bass just shook his head. Then he erupted. "Get the girl the hell out of here. See that she gets out of camp, Ned."

"I want to watch her go," Shell said. Kolka, not understanding any of this clung to Shell's sleeve anxiously, her eyes wide, her attention shifting from man to man.

"All right. Let's all step outside for a minute then."

She didn't want to go. Kolka was loyal, but with prodding and pushing, much sign language, she was finally convinced. Shelter watched her disappear into the rocks and vanish into the shadows beyond the camp.

A gun prodded Morgan in the ribs. "Now. You turn over that damned gold or it's over, understand?"

"It would be pretty hard not to," Shell said. "Come on. We've got a climb ahead of us."

They started up the hogback, Shelter, Joe Bass and two men. In half an hour, after a little casting about in the moonlit hills, Shell found the spot where he had buried the gold and he dug it up.

"Here." He dusted the saddlebags off and handed them to Joe Bass who didn't seem that interested all of a sudden. Bass passed them to Ned who was a little more eager to touch the ransom money.

"It looks like it's all here, Joe. Can't count it in this light, but if there's anything missing, it's not much."

"The horses," Joe Bass said stonily. He stood on the

154

broken ridge, the moonlight illuminating his youthful features. Shelter knew what he meant.

"No. Not just yet."

"Don't be a fool. Tell me where the horses are and you can take off—alive."

"We've got to have a talk first, Bass. And then, if I like your answers I'll give you back your horses."

"You'll give them back," Ned said sharply, "or I'll crack your skull for you."

"Easy, Ned," Bass said, though he looked like he wouldn't have minded cracking Shell's skull himself. "We're going to have to do it Morgan's way or not do it at all, the way it looks."

"You've got the ransom," Morgan said. "Are you going to turn Dorothy Patch loose now?"

"Why you damned fool . . ." Ned blustered.

Joe Bass was calmer. "You've seen her. You think she wants to leave me?"

"No. I guess not." Shell sat down on a rock, causing Ned's rifle to shift slightly. "She's not your real sister, after all."

"That's right, she's not."

"Joe," Ned said a little nervously. "I don't like being up on this ridge much. There's Indians around, you recollect."

"All right." Bass looked at Shell and decided that he looked too comfortable there. "Back down to the camp. There's a chance the boys found those ponies. Then we wouldn't have to deal with Mr. Morgan at all."

They hadn't gotten the horses. Two men had returned footsore and weary. "Can't track no damn horses in the dark. That Indian, or whoever it is that's got them ponies must know this territory blind."

155

"All right. Sit tight for a while. Start breaking camp," Bass instructed.

"We makin' for the border, Joe?"

"I hope so. With any luck."

"You got the money!"

"That's right." He nodded at Ned who held it up, "And I hope to have the horses soon. Now let's quit jabbering and get moving. The marshal can't be far behind."

The girl still stood in the tent. She was a pretty thing, Shelter thought. Fine golden hair spun its way down across her shoulders. Proud high breasts jutted against the fabric of the cotton shirt she wore.

"You two were in on this together," Shell said. It wasn't a question.

"That's right." Bass held a gun on Shell as Ned went through the saddlebags again, his lips moving as he counted the gold with fumbling fingers.

"All here, Joe."

"I thought so. Morgan doesn't care about the money. That's what he told us." Bass tilted back his hat. "The question is, what is Mister Morgan here for? What does he care about?"

"He came to rescue me," Dorothy Patch said. She stepped to where Joe Bass stood and she wrapped an arm around around his waist, kissing him on the cheek. "Right, Mister Morgan?"

"While I thought you wanted rescuing it seemed like a good idea."

"But that's not really what brought you out here."

"No. I want to talk about things. About your father."

Morgan was interrupted harshly, savagely by Dorothy Patch. "You want to know how it was, why we're running away! All right, I'll tell you and you can go back and

156

tell the rest of Jacumba, the rest of the world how it was with Joe and me. We've always cared for each other, always, and we knew we'd get married one day. We're brother and sister in law only. We've no blood relationship."

"I know that," Shell said.

The girl's eyes sparked now. The blood was rising in her, spotting her cheeks with crimson.

"But Mister John Patch wouldn't hear of it. Mister John Patch thought it was scandalous—or so he said. He made out that Joe was a bad one, accused him of things, hypocritically forgiving him at the same time—for things he'd never done!"

"So Joe changed his name?"

"That was all later. Later," Dorothy went on. "He tried making Joe out to be an outlaw. He tried to convince me, but it didn't work. I knew Joe better. Even after he had moved out I saw Joe every night. You know why the old man did it, don't you, Morgan? You can't be that dumb."

"Why don't you tell me," Shell prompted.

"Because the old bastard was groping me all the time I was growing up. Grabbing at me in the hallways, walking in on my baths. All those years—well, I could take it as long as I had Joe. Then when he drove Joe away I just couldn't take it any more!"

"So you worked up this kidnapping plan."

"That's right," Dorothy Patch said, tossing her head, sniffing a little. "We need money to live in Mexico. Joe didn't have any, I didn't have any of my own. The old skinflint has thousands and thousands of dollars in his safe. I thought it up, the kidnapping, and I talked Joe into it. It seemed the perfect revenge, you see? He had made

157

Joe into an outlaw—very well, then the outlaw Joe would rob him of his money."

Bass had stood by quietly during this and now he shook his head. "Maybe it was all a mistake."

"We've got the gold now, Joe. It's nothing to him! Nothing at all. You wouldn't have wanted me to stay with him, would you? Not one more day."

"No," Bass said, holding her to him. "Not one more day. I just don't want to think about it anymore. I don't want to talk about John Patch at all!"

"You satisfied now, Morgan?" Ned asked. "Now you gonna show us where those horses are?"

"No, I'm not quite satisfied. I need to talk to you, Joe. About your father."

"I said I was through talking about John Patch!"

"I mean your real father."

Bass looked at Morgan and laughed. "My real father—why, damn you, Morgan, who the hell do you think John Patch is?"

"I don't get you," Shell said, but all of a sudden he thought he did understand, understand it quite clearly.

"Yes. That's right. He told me I was adopted all these years. How the hell do you think that made me feel! He wouldn't even allow that I was his real son! All the people in Jacumba will tell you what a nice man John Patch is. Old John Patch, ain't he swell, adopted this little ragamuffin boy then turned around and took in a homeless girl. Hell yes he took me in—he was my father! Yes, he took Dorothy in, he wanted himself a play toy. My father, Mister Morgan, is not a nice man at all."

"But this business of calling yourself Joe Bass . . ."

"Nothing to it. I found the records my father kept in an old locked steel box. Found my birth certificate in there. I don't know what I was doing—I guess adopted kids always wonder about their real parents. Well, I found mine." Bass laughed sharply, a little wildly. "I found mine all right, and it was him that had adopted me."

"But he isn't John Patch."

"No, he isn't, there is no John Patch and never was. He adopted that name at the same time he "adopted" me. Hell, Morgan, you must know by now what I'm telling you. John Patch's real name is Joe Bass."

Shelter stood there looking at the kid, at the little traces of venom moving behind his eyes, at the angry lips, the clenched jaw. If you looked close enough you could see the resemblance to a long-ago man, a mocking, dark-haired man with skin stretched so taut across his cheek-bones that it looked like it might split.

"You knew it," the kid said.

"I guess I did, in a way," Shelter answered. "It was difficult to see Joe Bass underneath all that accumulated fat, with his hair gone snow white. But I guess I some-how knew—at least I knew that John Patch wasn't what he seemed to be."

"Why is he asking?" Dorothy asked, squinting at Shell as if he were far off. "Why does he want to know about Joe Bass?"

"Why do you, Morgan?"

Shelter shrugged. "I came to see that Joe Bass paid for something he did a long while back."

"Something terrible."

"Yes, Miss. Something horrible."

"Kill him," she hissed and even Joe Bass was shocked at the hatred in her voice. "The things he did to me, the things he made me do while we were growing up . . . kill him, Morgan, kill him!"

"No." Shell shook his head.

"But you said . . ."

159

"I said I came to see that Joe Bass paid for his crime. I did. But I'm not a murderer, Dorothy. I don't walk up to a man and execute him no matter what he did. I don't think a whole lot of the way the law works, at times I doubt the law and justice have much to do with one another, but I won't abandon the law to live like the animals do."

"Then how . . ."

"We've got enough on John Patch to put him away for the rest of his life—never mind what Major Joe Bass did long ago."

"What are you talking about?" Joe asked uneasily.

"I'm talking about what he did to Dorothy, what he did to you."

"And who's going to arrest him? Thornhill!"

"Thornhill's going down too. He's a kill-for-pay lawman and he's going to be exposed."

"You're going to do that too?"

"That's right."

Joe Bass laughed out loud and spun away, his hands rising skyward. "That's funny, Morgan. That really is funny."

"Is it? I'll tell you something that's not so funny. You'll never make the Mexican border. If you do make it you'll never survive down there. Patch will hire more people to come after you and they'll find you. They'll find you and kill you. You can run for a time, you can run but then that five thousand is going to run out. You're going to have to split it up anyway, with Ned and your other friends. It won't last long split up, and when the money runs out you'll be out there on that limb. In a foreign land with no money and the hunters on your trail. You'll live in fear the rest of your lives. You'll grow to hate each other, too. Blaming each other for what has happened to you. It's no life, it's a slow death making this run now."

"Shut up, Morgan!" Ned shrieked. "Shut up and tell us where the damned horses are."

But Joe Bass was thinking, standing there, his eyes meeting those of Dorothy Patch.

"If you go back the old man will be locked up. You'll have what's rightfully yours, the ranch, all that's locked up in that safe you were talking about."

"To hell with the ranch, to hell with the money," Joe Bass said.

"Joe, we can't . . ." Dorothy was clutching at his sleeve but he didn't seem to notice.

"Not the money, not the ranch. That's not what I want—but to see them close the cell door on John Patch, my father Major Joe Bass."

"It won't work. Joe, you're going crazy. Don't listen to this man. Have you forgotten what's outside there— Marshal Thornhill and his men, the wide desert. We don't have a chance." Dorothy's eyes were flooded with tears.

"It's what we should have done in the first place, don't you see?" He turned the girl's face up to his. "Morgan's right—the law must handle this. As for Thornhill and his men, why, we've got some good soldiers with us, right Ned?"

"If you say so, Joe," Ned said, hanging his head slightly.

"And we've got Morgan—isn't that right, Morgan?"

"If you're going back, Joe, I'll be right at your shoulder. You couldn't keep me out of it."

"If we're going back," Ned said unhappily, "let's get moving before I change my mind. Now, Morgan—Now can we have those damned horses back?"

"Now," Morgan replied with a grin, "you got 'em."

15.

Hanapa had the horses hidden up a narrow gorge. He led Shelter there, looking at him as if he was crazy. That was all right. Ned had been looking at Shell that way all night. By then Morgan wasn't sure they weren't right. He had carved himself out a big piece of trouble.

"There's two spare horses, Morgan," Joe Bass said. "Pick yourself one. I don't know what you were planning to do about the Indians."

Shelter didn't know either. They couldn't go with him back to Jacumba, they just couldn't. Hanapa knew it, and he knew enough to simply shake Shelter's hand, rest his other hand briefly on his shoulder and walk away, leaving Morgan and Kolka alone.

Shelter took her face in his hands, smiling down at her. The moonlight was on that face and the dark eyes were glossy as she looked up at him. It was tough, and her not understanding should have made it a little easier, but it didn't.

"Look, Kolka, I've got to go finish this job of mine. I know you'd understand if I could tell you in your own language. I'm a warrior, Kolka, and the battle is about to begin—I can't stay behind with my woman no matter how much I'd like to."

She didn't say a word, didn't curse him or jabber at him in the Kikima tongue. She took his right hand, kissed the palm of it and ducked under his arm to dart away toward her grandfather, the two of them vanishing moments later into the dark and shadows.

"You ready now, Morgan?" Ned asked. There was no mockery in the Texan's voice. Maybe he had left a woman behind him down his backtrail too.

"Ready. You got a rig for me?"

"A rig and a horse under it. I chose that dapple gray for you. Used to belong to a good man."

Shelter didn't ask what had happened to the man. He didn't want to tempt the fates by thinking about it. It was a long ride they had ahead of them across some rough country. They would be lucky to make it.

He looked at the girl, Dorothy Patch sitting her horse stiffly, looking extremely young as the moonlight revealed her unmarked, childish face. Hell, Joe Bass was nothing but a kid himself, two kids who had been stung by a dirty old bastard, a killer and consummate actor.

Shelter swung aboard the gray after adjusting the stirrups to his long legs.

"Ready?" Joe Bass asked.

"As ready as I'm going to get. Which way out of here?"

"There's a little trail through the hills to the north. It should be our best way. Thornhill was south of us. I don't

163

think he'd circle twenty miles around. I doubt he'd know about that pass anyway, not many do."

"And if he does?"

"You got your rifle back from that Indian girl, didn't you?" Joe Bass said grimly. "Well, hold on to it."

And it would come to that, Shell knew it now. Thornhill would have shown up at the spot where the ransom was to have been passed. He would have shown up and Joe Bass wouldn't have. Thornhill knew where the ransom money was and he seemed to be capable of adding two and two together.

If he knew about that pass, he would be there.

And if he didn't—well, that left him only seventy miles, two days and a night to catch up with Joe Bass. If he couldn't manage that there was Jacumba itself.

Shell had talked big enough about doing this right and legal, but the wish he had been spreading was a little thin if you examined it closely.

What did they have but the word of Joe and Dorothy against the old man's word? And Joe had been riding the outlaw trail. The girl—well she was hysterical, they might say, under Joe's influence. Then there was Thornhill. Morgan knew that he was a drunken killer, but that wouldn't cut much ice. It had to be proven.

"Ready?" Joe Bass asked, watching as Shell sat immersed in his own thoughts.

"I suppose so."

"Second thoughts?"

"Haven't you had a few?" Shell asked.

"You'd better believe it. Mister, I'm risking a rope or a prison term, risking that woman's happiness. What do you think I'm chewin' on?"

"I know it. Joe, all I told you about running to Mexico

164

is true. They'd track you down, boy, slit your throat."

"Yes. I know it's true. If it wasn't, well—I guess I'd be on my way south now. I'm not doin' this to please you, you know, Morgan."

"No. The old man," Morgan asked quietly, looking away from Bass, toward the moonshadowed mountains, "is there any feeling at all in you for him? Is it going to slow things up?"

"You mean if you decide to shoot him dead?" Joe Bass was smiling, but it wasn't a pretty thing to see. "Mister, I'd stand up and cheer. He wasn't my father—he was a man who got me one night when he was bored and drunk and dropped his pants."

"Don't let it eat you up inside, Joe."

"It don't eat anymore, Morgan. It ate and ate all the time I was growing up. Now I don't reckon there's anything left to eat. You can believe this though—whatever happens it's all right. If they hang him I won't be sobbing my little eyes out about it, I'll guarantee it. And if you have to shoot him, well, make sure that I'm there to see it."

Joe jerked his horse's head around angrily and they trailed out, Shell watching for a moment, wondering what that kid had endured, what Dorothy had been put through.

He fell in beside the last man, a quiet dark-haired cowboy he hadn't been introduced to. It was no time for talking and so they rode on silently up the canyons of the desert mountains, the moon at their backs, the peaks towering overhead. And away back behind somewhere, a young Indian woman standing, watching.

Fine dust rose high into the air, drifting lazily back above the column of night riders. It was enough. Enough for a good scout to smell, perhaps enough to see or hear as the hoofs clomped down on the hard-packed earth, clicked off the occasional stone, as the bridle chains jingled and leather squeaked. They rode as silently as they could, but all of these noises were there for the enemy to hear if he had the ears, the patience to lie still and listen, holding his own breath.

The Apache had that kind of patience if the others didn't, Morgan reflected.

"You shouldn't have talked Joe into this."

Dorothy Patch had ridden up alongside of Shell now. It was no time, no place for conversation, but from the look in her eyes, she had to get it off her mind, and she did.

"You're killing us, you know. Joe at least."

"No. It'll work out. It's the other way that was suicide."

"Wait, you'll see," she repeated. The woman was very rigid in the saddle, her eyes fixed straight ahead, it was a while before he recognized what he was seeing—extreme fear. She was literally scared stiff, nearly unable to move, so frightened was she of what they'd find in Jacumba.

"You can guarantee this, I suppose," she said brittily. "Guarantee that everything will go all right."

"Yes," Morgan said quietly. "I can guarantee it. I swear it to you, Dorothy, this will work out for the best. I'm behind that oath. My guns are behind it. I'll make sure the old man never gets you back, I'll guarantee that Joe Bass never goes to jail for crimes he hasn't done."

She slowly turned her head looking at Morgan, just looking, wanting to believe what he said, knowing that down inside he couldn't be any more sure than she was.

"Thanks," was all she said, then she urged her horse

166

on ahead to catch up with Joe Bass at the head of the column.

"Well, you gave that lady a load, didn't you?" the dark-haired cowboy asked. He thumbed his hat back, crossed his hands on the pommel and grinned at Shelter Morgan.

"Afraid so." The grin was infectious and Morgan returned it. "Shelter Morgan." He stuck out a hand.

"Yes. I've heard the name. And we've met before." The cowboy took off his hat. "Can you see it?" He fingered the bump.

"That's a goose egg you got there."

"It sure is," the man said, putting his hat back. "Know how it got there?"

"Sorry," Shell said. That was some of Morgan's night work.

"Hell, you could've killed me, couldn't you? A headache isn't much to go through if it gets Randy Patch back his property, gets the girl home safe and sound."

"You fellows think a lot of Joe Bass, don't you?"

"No. I think a lot of Randy Patch. I think he's gone just a little crazy, calling himself by his Pa's name . . . is that why his old man turned on him?"

"Sure. He couldn't have that name used. He knew sooner or later someone would hear that name," Shell said.

"Someone like you."

"That's right. Someone exactly like me."

"Do you figure the marshal will hit us?"

"What do you think?" Shell asked dryly.

"Yeah, I guess he will. I figure he had orders to kill the kid anyway."

"He did." Shell had heard those orders given. At the

time it had struck him as an old man's raving. It wasn't. Had Major Joe Bass recognized Shelter? Sure he had. And maybe word had gotten to the Campbells or Jack Claypool who was playing things very coolly as he always did. Jack Claypool who had a personal grudge at stake. Jack Claypool whose brother was lying dead in Texas, killed in battle by Shelter Morgan.

The moon was riding high in a cold, clear sky, the stars away from the moonglow were brilliant, huge. The party of horsemen dipped down toward the flats and they began to check their weapons, to shift gunbelts and mentally and physically count cartridges. Once on the flats they were visible for miles. And Jeb Thornhill couldn't let them go, he just couldn't. He had already participated in one massacre; he wasn't going to balk at another one.

"Ride easy, Morgan," Ned said from beside him.

"I've been riding easy for a long while, Ned."

"Yeah, I'll bet you have. What was you, an officer?" Ned was eyeing him speculatively.

"I didn't start out that way. I enlisted out of Tennessee. They gave me a field commission. I came out a captain."

"They didn't give me nothin' but a musket ball in the butt at Wilson's Creek. My war didn't last long."

"That's the only kind to have."

"No, sir," the Texan said, "a winning war is the only kind to have. Just go South and ask."

"Let's hope this one is both," Morgan said. "A short one and a winning one."

"Amen," Ned said and he tugged down on his hat, drifting away.

Everyone was a little tenser now. They rode on in silence, dark insects moving across the vast salt playas,

he rippling dunes to the south moving eerily in the light
reeze. There was frost in the hollows, creating bizarre,
nsubstantial lakes and ice forests in miniature among
he cactus. Then that would be gone and there was only
he flats again. Endless cracked, white, playa. A dead
ake, a dead sea where nothing would ever live again and
much had died. Ancient organisms gone with their time,
;one with the sea.

It would be a miracle if morning didn't leave more
leath strewn across the playa.

It came early. Morning grayed the skies briefly then
he sun blossomed in the east, a red flower bringing
;udden warmth to the desert. The moon, still high in the
;ky, gave up the unequal battle and paled to white.

And the long line of riders appeared to the south,
strung out across the horizon.

No one spoke. There was no need to. Heads turned
southward, knowing somehow before they were clearly
dentified that it was Thornhill and his hard men coming
o do murder.

Joe Bass rode up at a hard gallop, his rifle in his hand.
He reined to a stop beside Shelter, his horse going to hind
egs, hoofs pawing at the air.

"What do we do, Morgan. Stand them here?"

"No, they've got to catch us. Your horses should be
resher than Thornhill's. Let's make a run for it."

"Afraid to fight?" someone shouted.

"Tell you what," Shelter answered. "You stay here
and hold them off."

The man declined. Ned laughed out loud. Even Joe
Bass, tense as he was, managed a smile. He turned to the
men who rode with him, men who followed him out of
personal admiration.

169

"You heard Morgan. We're going to try to stay ahead of them. No sense forcing the fight."

Shell glanced southward. Thornhill seemed to be closing the gap with amazing quickness although the horses weren't being abused. They simply came on riding forward, dark silhouettes from out of the orange haze of sunrise.

"Switch Dorothy's saddle to the other spare horse," Morgan said.

"Now?"

"Yes, now. You want her on a fresh mount, don't you?" Morgan asked.

"Yes." Joe looked southward. There was no telling how things would run if they captured Dorothy. They were hard men with no respect for anything, not even the commands of their leaders. "Switch that saddle, will you, Ernie?"

"The gold can go on that mount," Shell coached. "Come on, let's keep moving."

He didn't need to urge them on. It was easy enough to glance southward and draw inspiration from the approaching line of marauders. The saddle was switched, Dorothy given a hand up and then they were off again, moving evenly across the desert, trying to maintain a pace just slightly faster than that of the outlaws.

The first shot was fired a mile on.

Whining across the flats it struck nothing. Shelter went low across his saddle. He wasn't alone. Glancing back he could see the puff of smoke rising above one rider.

"Impatient, ain't he," Ned cracked.

The foothills were miles distant. The sun beat down mercilessly. Shelter glanced back, feeling it, knowing

170

uddenly. They were losing ground to Thornhill's mob.

"We're not going to make it," Joe Bass said.

"Got any ideas?"

"Arroyo Seco."

"What's that?"

"Just a gulley cut into the flats. A mile and a half north. There's not much there, but we'd have cover if we can get there. Thornhill would still be up in the open."

"You want to stand and fight them here."

Joe Bass shrugged. "It's as good a place to die as any, I reckon."

"Yes," Shell looked briefly to the distances. "I guess it is."

They increased their own pace now, lifting the horses into a ground-devouring run. A screen of white dust lifted from the salt playa and drifted southward. More shots sounded distantly like small firecrackers, but no one was hit.

Shelter saw it suddenly. A deep gouge scoured into the white earth, a flaming gash winding across the playa. Arroyo Seco. A place to die.

The arroyo was a half a mile across, clotted with stands of tinder dry, gray willow and low thorny brush in some places, completely barren in others. A desolate cotton-wood tree lifted a gray, lifeless head skyward.

They hit the arroyo at the run, the horses sliding down the sandy banks, spraying up dust and sand. Shelter was from his saddle in seconds, scrambling back up the bank to elbow into a position beside Ned and Joe Bass.

"Look at 'em come," Ned whistled.

There was something almost mad about it. Thornhill's people were charging across the flats at a flat-out pace now, knowing that the guns were waiting for them. Or maybe they didn't; maybe they thought no one would dare to stand up against them and their vengeance guns.

"Hold it," Shell was saying softly. "Don't fire yet. Hold it . . ." but someone did fire, out of nervousness, fear, and the Thornhill gang spread wide, whipping their horses toward the flanks of Shelter's tiny army.

Shell saw Jack Claypool, tracked him with his sights for a fragment of a second and then lost him as the horse suddenly dipped low behind a veil of powder smoke. There was a lot of firing going on suddenly from both sides, though Shelter saw no one hit.

"Damnit, hold your fire! Hold your fire!"

They had already wasted their best chance with that early shot; there was no sense in burning up what little ammunition they had firing at phantoms. Shelter had seen war before and he knew how many rounds nervous soldiers could squeeze off.

"Where's the girl?" he shouted at Joe Bass.

"With the horses." Bass nodded a head back toward the willows.

"You get down there then and stay with her."

"I can handle my share of the fighting," Bass said angrily.

"Fine. Then I'll stay with the girl. Damnit, Joe, she needs someone watching her. What the hell's the use of any of this if they get her . . ." the rifle bullet sang past Shell's ear and he ducked his head. He jabbed a finger at Joe Bass. "You get down with her!"

"All right," Bass muttered and he turned angrily, sliding down the sandy bluff toward the horses.

"What now, General?" Ned asked.

"They're into the arroyo, Ned, it's a different fight. Get some people up to the north of us here. Keep to the bottom of the arroyo, but don't take your eyes off the rim. They'll try to come over on us."

"All right." Ned took two men with him and started north. Shell tapped the puncher on the other side of him and started him off toward the south with the same instructions. Then he settled in behind the sights of his Winchester, waiting for the frontal attack which was bound to come, waiting and watching for Death which was going to come sweeping across the desert flats.

16.

The bullet whined past Shelter's head and was joined by a dozen others. The crackling of the rifles to the north and south showed that it was a concerted, thoughtful attack. Thornhill's people weren't the kind of greenhorns Shell had.

The first horseman appeared incredibly near at hand as if the man and animal had risen out of the sands to fight. The man was a dark faced, lean kid with a red scarf around his neck. He died without a sound as the .44-40 bullet went in beneath his chin and exited high up, taking most of the skull and all of the kid's brains with it. Any ambitions the kid had had, dreams, memories, ideas of courage or of profit were spread across the desert flats, and Shelter switched his sights, not wasting the time feeling sorrow for a man who had come hunting death on the desert and found it.

To Shell's left two horsemen came over the rim of the sandy arroyo. One of Shelter's men went down beneath the hoofs of the horse nearest. The second horse went down on its side, kicking, whinnying as Morgan's rifle punched led through its heart. Men dove out of the thrashing horse's way and scattered into the brush as a second wave of attacking cavalry came out of the salt flats to attack their position.

Shell could hear heavy fire to the north, lighter fire to the south. Suddenly he saw something nearer at hand, something which gave him a shot of adrenalin, a moment's intense satisfaction.

Hector Campbell. Hector Campbell afoot, running down the sandy bluff to Shell's right, firing into the brush with a handgun, his dull face set in a murderous little smile.

Shelter settled the bead sight on the big man's chest and fired. One down. Hector Campbell pitched face forward into the sand and stayed there.

Three horsemen breached the defenses to the south suddenly and were charging up the canyon. Shelter saw them ride over one of his men, guns blazing. Simultaneously two more riders appeared in front of him. One of them was the Apache.

Shell's sights picked up the first horse and fired, taking the heart out of it. The bay rolled, spilling its rider. Then he fired quickly, too quickly, in the direction of the Apache. Missed. He fired again, the horse nearly on top of him.

The Apache's horse was hit and Shell rolled aside, seeing the Apache leap free. The horse came between them, a flailing, mortally wounded thing dying for a cause it never understood.

175

The Apache was into the brush, knife in hand, moving away from Shell. Morgan was to his feet in a second, dashing across the open ground, bullets digging up sand at his heels. Then he was into the heavy brush, crouching, listening and watching.

He didn't have to wait, not for the Apache. A shadowy blur caught the corner of Shell's eye and he flung himself backward to land against the sand as the Apache swiped at his head with his rawhide-handled knife.

Shell's rifle flew free, losing itself in the brush and Morgan drew his own bowie, coming to his knees to meet the second savage assault of the Apache.

The Indian's knife struck downward violently, but Shell managed to get his own knife up. Steel rang against steel. The Apache's eyes were feral, savage. He wanted to kill—not because he had to. He wanted it. Wanted to taste blood, to see Morgan's disembodied heart.

He wasn't good enough.

He just wasn't good enough. He grabbed Shell's wrist and yanked his own knife back again, ready to strike down with the fatal blow.

Morgan had his own ideas about that. He reached up from the ground and yanked the Apache downward by his shirtfront. Shell's forehead crashed into the Indian's face, breaking his nose, spraying them both with blood. The Indian struck out wildly with his knife, in anger, in blood lust. But something had gone wrong and it was a horrifying second later that he realized what had happened.

Morgan's big bowie was buried to the hilt in the Indian's gut, the tip of the knife touching the heart, rupturing it. The Apache writhed violently on the knife, wanting to kill, wanting to lift his own knife which was

176

buried in the sand inches from Morgan's head one more time, to strike out, to kill.

Pain flooded his chest, violent, sledge-hammer pain and he knew. The Apache's face went blank and he slumped forward to lie inert, blood-soaked against Morgan.

Shell rolled the dead man aside and yanked his knife free. He found his rifle in the brush and started away, back toward the bluff.

The scream turned him around quickly.

"Dorothy." It was Dorothy Patch, and the scream was one of absolute terror. If they had gotten to her then they had gone over Joe Bass. Smothering a curse Shelter started through the tangled brush on the run. The willow branches whipped at his face and arms. He stumbled on. A second scream came on the heels of the first and Shelter broke into a dead run.

He was suddenly out of the brush and into the middle of a struggle. Joe Bass lay on the sand, writhing while a horse, riderless, wounded itself, reared over him. Across the empty patch of sand to Shelter's left stood Dorothy Patch, twisting, crying, fighting back as Jeb Thornhill pawed at her, tearing her dress free of her shoulders and milk-white breasts. Beside and one step behind the marshal was the bulky, red-bearded Sam Campbell. His florid face was placid, somehow uglier for being so unemotional at a moment like that.

"Campbell!" Shelter called out. The big man started to make his turn, his eyes widening as he saw the tall, blue-eyed man, saw the big Colt in his hand. Campbell started to bring his gun to bear, but it was too slow. Shelter cut loose, dropping to a knee to fire twice, the .44 bucking against his palm.

The first shot lifted the huge form of Sam Campbell to his toes, the second caved him in, digging a hole through his blubbery gut, the red hot .44 slug shattering his spine as it exited, spraying blood across the willow brush behind him.

Shelter was already moving. He had chosen Campbell as his first target, and that might have been a mistake. Jeb Thornhill had shoved the girl away from him, drawn his pistol and fired even as Shelter watched Campbell go down.

Only the fact that Morgan was already rolling away saved him from being punctured by lead from the marshal's six-gun. Shelter saw the savage hatred in the marshal's eyes, the incredible anger and then the sudden pain as a gunshot echoed in Morgan's ear.

The marshal's face was contorted with agony as the blood smeared his shirt front. Thornhill slapped at his chest, trying desperately to stem the flow, but it was no use. Blood pumped between his fingers and flooded his clothing. He looked at Morgan with wide, red-edged eyes and then looked behind Shell.

"You filthy little . . ."

He never finished that. He simply folded up like an unstrung marionette and collapsed. Shelter looked behind him then, seeing Joe Bass on his knees, blood smearing his forehead, the still-smoking Remington pistol in his two hands.

"Got the bastard, didn't I?" Joe asked and Shell nodded.

"You got him, Joe. Take it easy now."

"I got the bastard," Joe Bass repeated. "Guess I . . ." then he toppled forward, and Dorothy screamed again, rushing toward them, forgetting that her dress was ripped off her above the waist, not caring as she knelt beside Shelter who was fingering the kid's scalp.

"Well?" Dorothy asked in despair.

"It's nothing much," Shell was able to tell her. "The bullet took off a patch of scalp but that seems to be all. He'll live to marry you, I guess."

"Shelter . . ." Joe Bass started to talk, and Shell didn't want to have the kind of conversation they were set to have.

"Forget it," Morgan said a little roughly. "Keep your gun in your hand. I'm going to see what the hell Ned's got."

The firing had fizzled, becoming sporadic then stopping altogether. He found Ned and the dark-haired puncher together. "Where's everyone else? What's happening?"

"Nothing's happening," Ned said, turning a powder-smoke blackened face to Shell. "Everyone just gave it up." He nodded down the slope then and Shell saw three dead men, beyond the rim of the arroyo another man lying broken, twisted on the desert flat.

"Let's count heads," Morgan said, taking charge. You had to keep it business-like or it just got to you, turning your belly upside down.

Ned, Joe Bass, the girl, the dark-haired puncher with the goose egg on his head. They were all that were left.

The outlaw gang had been devastated. Ned thought a couple of them had gotten away, but Shell found two he didn't know, four he knew too well. Both Campbell brothers and Jeb Thornhill were dead. The Apache was dead.

Joe Bass was on his feet again, Dorothy with him. She had found a couple of pins somewhere, enough to hold her dress up in front.

"We did it," Bass said numbly. "The bastards are dead."

"Yeah." Shell, who had been burying the dead, wasn't sure that anyone had won. "Let's get our horses gathered and get on out of here. We've got a long ride to Jacumba."

"Going on with it, are we?" Ned asked.

"Why, sure, Ned," Joe Bass replied, putting a hand on the cowboy's shoulder. "Why wouldn't we go on? We've got him on the run now."

"Do we? Suppose we get there and the old man just tells you all to go to hell? Suppose he's got a few men with him and they find out we killed a marshal? Suppose they unkink a new rope and see if they can't make a loop that fits our necks?"

"It could happen," Joe Bass said. He looked at Morgan who could only shrug. "Are you saying that you want to pull off, Ned? I'd give you a cut of the gold, you and Andy."

"Hell, no," Ned said gruffly. He turned away, grabbing the dangling reins to his horse. "Damn it, Joe, I was just supposin'—you know me."

"Sure. I know you. Thanks, Ned. What about you, Andy?" he asked the dark-haired puncher.

"Hell, Joe, I don't speak no Mex. I'd better just tag along with you and see how she kicks."

"Morgan?"

Shelter smiled thinly, rubbing his arm. "Mister—you couldn't *keep* me from going along. Not now. I want that man who's sitting up there in his easy chair, staring at the fire, thinking his little evil thoughts, telling everyone what a fine, fine man he is. I want him—and he's mine,

Joe. You remember that if it comes down to it. He's all mine, is Major Joe Bass."

The dead lay beneath the sands. The living rode out half an hour later, leading a string of empty ponies. They rode in silence through the afternoon, and at evening they camped at the pond where Thornhill had led them on the way out. Shell sat apart from the fire, sipping his coffee, watching the dark and empty land. No one was feeling sociable though Joe and Dorothy sat shoulder to shoulder near the low fire.

The smell of gunpowder stayed in your nostrils for a while, the taste of death clung to the palate, taking away your appetite for much else. No one wanted to talk or eat; no one would be sleeping very well tonight.

It was only the death of their friends that bothered them, however; not the death of scum like the Campbells or Jeb Thornhill, men who killed to have a few extra dollars to drink away some Saturday night. At least Shell felt that way—the world was better rid of them.

In the morning he meant to make the world still a better place.

They saddled with the dawn, sipped a smoking cup of coffee and rode out, the horses breathing steam in the first cold hour.

By the time the sun had shaken off its mantle of color and clawed its way into the empty sky, the party had made the rocky foothills east of Jacumba and was climbing above the desert floor. They topped out the range and began walking their horses through the dry grass valleys which were spotted between those rock-clad hills. Joe looked around him as he rode with an expression Shelter couldn't quite make out. The kid was coming home, but home was something new, different now. He looked,

181

Shelter thought, a little disgusted.

"Hold it a while," Shelter said as they approached the knoll which overlooked the valley where the white house stood.

"What are you talking about? Why stop now?"

"He just might not be alone."

"Of course he's alone—outside of Manta and a few older hands."

"Not if he got the word that you've killed Thornhill," Shelter said.

"How could he . . . ? Oh."

"Yeah, oh. Two men, Ned says. Two men got out of that firefight down on the desert. One of them was Jack Claypool, and I guarantee you he didn't run. He doesn't know how. No, he came back to settle with the boss, to see how they can go about winning this little set-to."

"Let's have us a look," Ned said and he and Shell rode up to the crest of the knoll, veering off the trail to emerge beneath a stand of great live oaks.

They sat looking down for a long while, studying the ranch and its environs. "If they're down there I can't make 'em out. Think those men had time to ride to town and get more guns anyway?" Ned asked.

"If they wanted to bad enough, and there's plenty at stake here. They weren't going to be worried about sparing the horses."

"Well, I don't see nobody."

"Neither do I." Shell squinted into the sunlight. "Where do you reckon they'd be if they *were* there, Ned?"

"I don't know. The barn, I suppose. Maybe upstairs in the house—they'd know we wanted the old man. Then in the oaks along the road, wantin' to cut off any escape route. Them three places."

"All right. That's where they are. That's the way we'll play it."

"Morgan," Ned said, looking at Shell in wonder, "you surely hate this man don't you?"

"That's right, Ned. If you'd seen what I did, you'd hate him too. I hate him enough to go through what I have twice, turn around and stump through hell to get Joe Bass. I only hope he tries something most foolish. I only hope that he tries to gun me, Ned, because then he's mine, all mine and I'll have him."

Ned sat his horse watching the tall, blue-eyed man, wondering what private devils kept him going, kept him hunting. He wondered how he slept at nights. He knew one thing—he was glad he hadn't been born with the name of Joe Bass. He wouldn't have wanted Shelter Morgan on his back trail.

"Well?" Shell said. "Do we go on in?"

"We go on in," Ned said, and they started their horses back toward the rest of their party, checking the loads in their guns as they rode.

17.

They came through the trees and sat in a line facing the house. Ned had been wrong with one guess—there were no soldiers in the trees along the road. Looking down at the house it seemed to be empty, seemed to have been empty for years.

They sat watching, waiting. There were no extra horses anywhere, none that could be seen or heard.

"He's pulled out," Andy guessed. No one was ready to agree with him.

"Let's hope not," Joe Bass said in a tight voice, the strain very evident now. "Dorothy, you'd better stay here."

"I'm going in," she said firmly. "No one's going to shoot a woman. Not John Patch's daughter. I'm what this is all about, remember?"

"I remember," Joe said. He knew it wasn't going to do

184

much good to argue with her.

"Ready?" Shell asked, and at Joe's nod he cocked his Winchester and started his horse forward from beneath the oaks. Shell's eyes moved from point to point constantly, checking the roof of the house, the barn and stable beyond the house, the rocks up beyond the breaking corral. All of it was still. Empty and still—it was far too still, Shell thought. He knew they were there. No jays bobbed in the trees, no insects hummed in the warm grass. Every door, every window was shut tight in the big house.

"The loft!" Ned shouted and Shell bailed out, leaping from his saddle to hit the ground and roll away toward the concrete watering trough as two rifles began firing from the loft of the barn.

Ned was the one to be hit, the bullet striking high, slapping him from the saddle as he grabbed at his chest. He went down hard, his horse dancing away in confusion. Andy had stuck the spurs to his pony and had made it to the stable where he dismounted on the run, drawing quite a bit of fire, but apparently not getting himself hit.

Joe and Dorothy sprinted for the house. No shots were aimed that way—the girl had been right about that, they were under orders not to hit her, and they couldn't shoot at Joe without chancing a hit on the girl.

There were no such orders concerning Shelter Morgan. He lifted up from behind the trough, trying to spot Ned, and the rifles opened up, chipping at the concrete trough, blasting cement dust into Morgan's eyes.

He answered with some .44s of his own, pumping the shells through that Winchester until the barrel was hot, splintering the frame around the loft, driving the outlaws back. Then Shell was up, moving in a crouch toward Ned, grabbing him by the shirt collar, towing him back toward the safety of the trough as he fired his Colt with his free hand, keeping the boys in the barn at bay.

Ned looked up, gratitude on his ashen face.

"How's it look, Morgan?"

"Nothing to it," Shell said, eyeing the dangerous chest wound. He couldn't do a damn thing about it just then. Ned would make it or he wouldn't, that was all.

The scream brought Shell's head up and around. Ned handed Shelter his own six-gun and said, "Go, General!"

Shelter grinned. He emptied his own Colt at the loft then made a dash for the house, the rifle bullets splintering the steps behind and beside his boots as he darted toward and through the empty doorway.

The badman stood there with a grin on his face and a shotgun in his hands. On the floor beside him lay Joe Bass. What he expected Shelter to do Morgan never knew. Stop maybe, put up his hands and surrender?

It was no time to play things that way. Morgan rolled to one side, triggering three times. The Colt spat flame and lead, slamming the outlaw back against the davenport behind him as the shotgun leaped in his hands, gouting flame. Buckshot ripped up a section of the oak flooring and started a fire smoldering in the cushions of what had been a chair.

Shelter dragged himself to his feet and started toward Joe Bass. The kid was all right apparently, someone had just knocked him silly. The old scalp wound was double-sized now and although Joe's eyes were open and he was trying to get to his feet, there wasn't much comprehension in his eyes. He was like a fighter just getting up after taking a long, long count.

"Sit down, Joe. You're not helping anyone." Shell put

him down, and roughly. He crept to the window, and peering out through the curtains saw that Andy had the barn well covered from his position in the facing stable. He had gotten at least one of them. A man lay sprawled beneath the loft, unmoving.

Shelter could see Ned behind the trough, but he couldn't tell how he was doing, alive or dead. He turned back to Joe Bass who was sitting on the chair, shaking his head.

"Where's your father? Where's Dorothy? What happened, Joe?"

Joe mumbled a few things that didn't make a bit of sense and then bowed his head, holding it on his knees. Shell patted his shoulder and moved on through the house, looking, listening, a cat on his feet.

He had come too far to screw this up now, and he didn't intend to. Outside Andy had forced a stalemate. Inside that wasn't good enough. It had to be won. The man had to resign the game or go down in a bloody defeat.

Shelter moved into the kitchen. Copper pots hanging neatly along one wall, the counters and sinks scrubbed neatly. The housekeeper, Theresa, stood against the back wall, her eyes wide with fear, her hands to her lips. Tears streamed down her cheeks. She glanced only once at Shell then stood staring at the door opposite.

Morgan, bloody, dusty, shirt torn, crossed the room, Colt at the ready, and the woman gave a tiny, fearful moan. He didn't ask her a thing, just followed her eyes.

He stood beside the door a second and then kicked it open. Bullets cut the lintel overhead and pinged off through the kitchen knocking pots and pans from their wall hooks.

"I've got the girl, Captain Morgan!" a voice boomed

out. "I've got the girl, and I'll kill her."

"Your own daughter?" Shell responded. He had to say something, keep the man talking while he figured this out. "You wouldn't hurt your own daughter. Let her go."

"No. She's not my blood. Besides, she turned her back on me, didn't she? Turned on me and ran off with that bastard Randy."

"Bastard?" Shell eased up closer and peered around the frame of the door. He couldn't see Major Joe Bass, but he could see his shadow. The sun was shining through a window at his back, painting shadows before the old man. Two shadows—his and the girl's who was struggling in his arms. Bass had acted like a sick, dying man. Maybe he was, but he had strength in those arms, the strength to hold Dorothy. "Bastard is a funny word for you to use about your own son, Major."

"So he told you all of that, did he? Listen, Morgan, this is no good. I can't come out and you can't come in. Let's talk a deal?"

Stalling. He was stalling but what for? "Sure, Major, let's talk." The shadows hadn't moved. Dorothy had quit wriggling now and was standing slack in his arm.

"This doesn't have to end in death. One of us will die, you know. Why? What for? I've got money enough for the two of us."

Stalling.

"No deal, Major. There's too many others who got cheated out of their share, a long time back, down along the Conasauga."

"Yes, but, Morgan—listen to me . . ."

Stalling. Then the breeze from the open back door stirred the copper kettles on the wall. It stirred them so that two of them clinked together softly and Shelter

188

Morgan ducked and turned as the bullets sprayed the wall above his head, showering him with plaster.

Shelter fired from where he was. The bullet punched through the flimsy wooden counter in front of him and took Jack Claypool in the groin. He screamed with pain and went down.

"Did you get him, Jack? Did you get the son of a bitch?" Major Joe Bass was eager. Very eager. He let go of the girl and rushed to the doorway. Shelter Morgan was standing there watching back. Shell hoped the major had time to look down the backtrail, to remember those that had died because of him, those that had frozen and starved—he hoped he had had that much time before the pistol barked and the white-haired, incredibly fat man buckled up and went down flat on his face against the kitchen floor.

Blood was beginning to leak out from under the body when Shell stepped across the dead man and took the smoking pistol from Dorothy Patch's hand.

"I got him," she kept repeating. "I actually killed the son of a bitch. I never really thought anything could hurt him, but I got the son of a bitch."

Morgan walked to where Jack Claypool lay moaning against the floor, holding his groin which was an exploded mess. Blood was everywhere. The bullet must have fragmented going through the counter and it had hit Claypool like jagged shrapnel.

"It wasn't the money," Jack managed to gasp. "It was family, you know? You killed my brother. How could I just forget it?"

"You should have forgotten it, Jack. You just should have," Morgan answered. It was another minute of horrible agony before Jack Claypool lay still in a pool of his own blood.

Shelter led Dorothy to the living room where young Joe Bass seemed to be coming around. He sat the two of them together, wondering if either would ever be the same again. Then he got a rifle from a rack on the wall and settled in at the window to help Andy clean up the snipers in the barn.

It was already taking on the haziness of memory when Shelter told it all to Merri Richardson over dinner that night. She listened awestruck to the tale of carnage and vengeance, her pretty head shaking from side to side with disgust.

"Well, he's dead now," she said, "and it's over. That is if things like that ever end for the kids who grew up in a house like that."

"He's a tough one is Joe Bass—he's going back to calling himself Randy Patch, by the way—he's tough and so is Dorothy. I guess they'll make it together."

"I saw the doctor upstairs. Ned will be all right, though he'll be in bed for a while."

"What about us?" Shell asked.

"What about us, what?" Merri asked, leaning forward, her chin on her fist.

"What about us being in bed for a while?"

"I thought you'd never ask."

"What about dinner?"

"Pork chops. Shall we simply tell the waiter to stuff them?"